STRAWBERRY GIRL

Strawberry Girl

written and illustrated

by

LOIS LENSKI

A YEARLING BOOK

Published by
DELL PUBLISHING CO., INC.
1 Dag Hammarskjold Plaza
New York, N.Y. 10017

Reprinted with arrangement with
J. B. Lippincott Company

ISBN: 0-440-48347-6

Printed in U. S. A.

Thirteenth Dell Printing—April 1977

For
two little Florida friends,
Betty Anne King
and
Barbara Smith

Picture
Map
of
Florida

⊡ Galloway —
Strawberries first
grown here

CONTENTS

FOREWORD

FEW people realize how new Florida is, or that, aside from
the early Indian and Spanish settlements, Florida has grown
up in the course of a single man's lifetime. In the early 1900's,
the date of my story, Florida was still frontier country, with vast
stretches of unexplored wilderness, woodland and swamp, and
her towns were frontier towns thirty and forty years later than
the same frontier period in the Middle West.

After the Seminole War, 1835-1842, Anglo-Saxons from the
Carolinas, Georgia and West Florida drifted south and took up
land in the lake region of Florida. Then began a bitter struggle
with the environment. Their descendants, in the second and
third generation, were, in 1900 and the following decade, just
prior to the coming of the automobile, living in a frontier com-
munity, with all its crudities, brutalities and cruelties. The
"Crackers" lived a primitive life, an endless battle went on—a
conflict with nature, with wild life, and with their fellow men.
Their life was replete with drama, and being people of character and dignity, they lived it, and still live it, with vigor.

[x]

Like their antecedents in the Carolina mountains, the Florida Crackers have preserved a flavorsome speech, rich in fine old English idiom—word, phrase and rhythm. Many old customs, folk songs and superstitions have been handed down along with Anglo-Saxon purity of type, shown in their unusual beauty of physical feature, and along with their staunch integrity of character.

Here then, in the Florida backwoods, a world exists, which few people, town residents or northern tourists, see, realize or even suspect. Many who see it fail sadly to understand it. Here is a real and authentic corner of the American scene, a segment of American life.

In this series of regional books for American children, I am trying to present vivid, sympathetic pictures of the real life of different kinds of Americans, against authentic backgrounds of diverse localities. We need to know our country better; to know and understand people different from ourselves; so that we can say: "This then is the way these people lived. Because I understand it, I admire and love them." Is not this a rich heritage for our American children?

My material has been gathered personally from the Crackers themselves, and from other Floridians who know and understand them. I have visited in Cracker homes. I have made many sketches of people, animals, the natural surroundings, their homes—plans, furnishings and details. I have come to know, understand and respect many of these people, and to number them among my friends. All the characters in my book are imag-

[xi]

inary, but practically all incidents used were told to me by people who had experienced them. Many were too dramatic for my purpose and had to be softened; some had to be altered to fit into my plot. To merit the confidence these people spontaneously placed in me has been a rich experience indeed.

I have consulted the WPA Florida Guide Book; The History of Polk County; Florida in the Making by Stockbridge and Perry; Palmetto Country by Stetson Kennedy; Four Centuries of Florida Ranching and other volumes.

I wish to extend my thanks to many Florida friends, among them members of the Sorosis Club in Lakeland, for their generous help.

Lois Lenski

LAKELAND, FLORIDA—Winters of 1942-43 and 1943-44
GREENACRES, HARWINTON, CONNECTICUT—Summer and
Fall of 1944

STRAWBERRY GIRL

"BIRDIE BOYER"

PROLOGUE

Trouble

"THAR goes our cow, Pa!" said the little girl.

"Shore 'nough, that do look like one of our cows, now don't it?"

The man tipped his slat-backed chair against the wall of the house. He spat across the porch floor onto the sandy yard. His voice was a lazy drawl. He closed his eyes again.

"She's got our markin' brand on her, Pa. A big S inside a circle," said Essie.

The man, Sam Slater, looked up. "Shore 'nough, so she has."

"She's headin' right for them orange trees, Pa," said Essie.

"Them new leaves taste mighty good, I reckon," replied her father. "She's hungry, pore thing!"

A clatter of dishes sounded from within the house and a baby began to cry.

"You'd be pore, too, did you never git nothin' to eat," said the unseen Mrs. Slater.

There was no answer.

The sun shone with a brilliant glare. The white sand in the

yard reflected the bright light and made the shade on the porch seem dark and cool.

"She might could go right in and eat 'em, Pa," said the little girl. Her voice was slow, soft and sweet. Her face, hands and bare legs were dirty. At her feet lay some sticks and broken twigs with which she had been playing.

Pa Slater did not open his eyes.

"Pa," Essie went on in a more lively tone, "iffen that cow laps her tongue around the new leaves, she'll twist the bark loose and pull it off. Do we not stop her, she might could eat up all them orange trees."

The man spat, then resumed his dozing position. "I don't reckon so," he said slowly.

❦❦❦❦❦❦❦❦❦❦❦❦❦❦❦❦❦❦❦❦❦❦❦❦❦❦❦

"Iffen she goes in that orange grove, them new folks will . . ."

The legs of the man's chair came down on the porch floor with a thump. He opened his eyes. "What new folks?"

"Them new folks what moved in the ole Roddenberry house," said Essie.

"New folks in that big ole house? Who tole you?" His staring gray eyes fixed themselves on the pale blue ones of his daughter.

"Jeff done tole me," said Essie. Although she was only seven, she was not afraid of her father. "They been here most a month already. They come in a big wagon. They moved in while you was away, Pa. We watched 'em unload."

"You did, eh?" growled Pa Slater. "You let 'em see you?"

"No." Essie smiled knowingly. "We hid in the palmettos, Pa. We got us a tunnel to hide in."

Her father grinned back at her. "Who be they?"

"Jeff says . . ."

Mrs. Slater, within, interrupted. "Name's Boyer. The man's a Caroliny feller."

"Why ain't you done tole me?"

" 'Cause you been gone away for so long."

"Got kids?" asked Slater.

"Regular strawberry family, jedgin' from the size of it—six or seven young uns, I reckon."

Mrs. Slater's reply was followed by the clatter of dishes and the crying of the baby. A smaller girl, about five, came out and climbed up on her father's lap.

[3]

"They got a gal . . ." began Essie. She looked at her father's frowning face and paused. In her mind she carried a bright picture of the new Boyer girl whom she hoped to have for a friend. She did not want it spoiled.

"Pa, our cow's done gone in their grove," she said again. "I'll go chase her out." She started down the steps.

"You come right back here and set down, young un," called Slater. "Let that cow go where she's a mind to." He tipped his chair back again lazily and closed his eyes.

"She might hurt them orange trees," ventured Essie, "and make trouble for us, Pa."

"Then they'll know they got neighbors!" Pa spat, and a wide grin spread over his face.

"Trouble!" he added softly. "You mighty right, gal young un. That skinny little ole cow's jest bound to make trouble!"

CHAPTER I

Callers

IT was a bright morning in early April. Birds were chirping and singing in the shady trees. A barelegged ten-year-old girl came out on the front porch. She watered the plants in the lard buckets there. She picked off a dead leaf or two.

"Ma!" she called. "The pink geranium's a-bloomin'. Come see it. Hit shore is purty!"

❦❦❦❦❦❦❦❦❦❦❦❦❦❦❦❦❦❦❦❦❦❦❦❦❦❦❦❦

Mrs. Boyer came out, drying her hands on her apron.

"Come down here, Ma, and look," begged the girl.

The woman came down the steps and stood at her side. The girl's brown hair was braided in two braids, looped up. Her eyes were big in her pointed face. She looked much like her mother.

"Ain't them right purty, Ma? I jest got to come out first thing in the mornin' and look at 'em."

"Purty, yes!" agreed her mother. "But lookin' at posies don't git the work done." She hurried back up the steps.

"Did I get some blue paint and paint the lard buckets, Ma, they'd look a sight purtier, wouldn't they?"

"Blue lard buckets!" laughed the woman. "Never heard of sich as that!" She disappeared in the house.

The girl took up a long broom made of brush—branches from a tree—and swept the yard clean. Its hard smooth surface felt good to her feet. Then she knelt in the path and began to set a row of bricks at an angle, to make a neat border. "I'll plant my amaryllis bulbs in the flower bed right here," she said to herself.

She stood up, her arms akimbo.

"Land sakes, somebody's comin'!" she called. "Ma! Callers!"

"Law me!" cried Mrs. Boyer, peeping out. "The Slaters! And my breakfast dishes not done."

The girl stared at the little procession.

Mrs. Slater, tall, thin and angular, carrying her baby like a sack of potatoes on her hip, was followed by the two little girls, Essie and Zephy. Some distance behind, as if curious yet half-unwilling to be one of the party, came a lanky twelve-year-old

[6]

❦❦❦❦❦❦❦❦❦❦❦❦❦❦❦❦❦❦❦❦❦❦❦❦❦❦❦❦

boy wearing a broad-brimmed black felt hat. The woman and children plowed the loose, dry sand with their bare feet. With each step forward, they seemed to slip a trifle backward, so their progress was slow. Bushy scrub oaks and a thicket of palmetto grew on the far side of the rough path, while a forest of tall pines rose in the distance.

The old Roddenberry house was not old enough to deserve to be called old. It had been built in the 1880's, the earliest type of Florida pioneer home. Deserted by the Roddenberrys after the Big Freeze of 1895, it had stood empty for some years, but showed few signs of neglect. The sturdy pine and cypress wood which had gone into its making were equal to many more years of Florida sun, rain, wind and heat.

The house was a simple one, but by backwoods standards a mansion. It was a double-pen plank house, with an open hall or breezeway in the middle. On one side was a bedroom, on the other the kitchen. Behind were two small shed rooms used for sleeping quarters. Wide porches spread across front and back.

The Slaters approached the picket fence timidly, staring with all eyes. Mrs. Slater opened the gate.

"Howdy!"

The girl in the path spoke first.

"Hey!" came the feeble response.

The girl tipped her head and smiled. "My name's Birdie Boyer," she said. "Come in and see Ma."

She led the way onto the front porch and across the breezeway. The boy did not come in.

"Can I borrow a cup o' sugar, ma'am?" inquired Mrs. Slater.

"Shore can!" said Mrs. Boyer heartily. "Ary time you need somethin', you call on me and welcome. That's what neighbors is for. Mighty nice to be near enough for neighborin'."

They sat down stiffly. An awkward silence fell.

"We had sich a heap o' work to do, to git this ole place fixed up," began Mrs. Boyer. "We ain't what you might call settled yet. Them Roddenberrys . . ."

"They got froze out in the Big Freeze," said Mrs. Slater. "They went back to wherever it was they come from. All their orange trees got bit back to the ground by the frost. Ain't no use messin' with oranges here. Hit's too cold in the wintertime."

"But the trees were seedlings," said Mrs. Boyer, "and they've come up again from the roots. When we git 'em pruned good and the moss cleaned out, they'll make us a fine grove."

"I got me a orange tree," said Birdie, " 'bout so high." She raised her hand to a height of about three feet. "I planted a bunch of seeds from an orange once. This seedling was the strongest —it come from the king seed. We brung it along with us and I planted it where the water drips from the pump. Soon I'll be pickin' my own oranges!"

"Yes, soon we'll be pickin' oranges to sell," added her mother.

"To sell?" asked Mrs. Slater in surprise.

"Yes, ma'am. We're studyin' to sell oranges and strawberries and sweet 'taters and sich and make us a good livin'."

"Sell things? Messin' with things to sell?" said Mrs. Slater. "Then you'll purely starve to death. Why, nothin' won't grow

[8]

here in Floridy. The only way we-uns can git us a livin' is messin' with cows and sellin' 'em for beef."

"We're studyin' to always have us a few cows too, and cow-pen the land. We git real benefit from our cattle, usin' 'em for beef and fertilizer, and for milk and butter too," said Mrs. Boyer.

"Why, them scrubby little ole woods cows don't give enough milk to bother with milkin' 'em," laughed Mrs. Slater.

"Where we come from," said Mrs. Boyer slowly, "we *feed* our cows."

"Feed 'em!" Mrs. Slater laughed a shrill laugh. "With all the grass they is to eat? Where you folks come from anyway?"

❦❦❦❦❦❦❦❦❦❦❦❦❦❦❦❦❦❦❦❦❦❦❦❦❦❦❦❦❦❦

"We come from Marion County last month," said Mrs. Boyer. "We come there in a covered wagon from Caroliny 'bout ten year ago."

Silence fell. Mrs. Slater's girls stared, tongue-tied, at the new girl.

"What's the matter with 'em, ma'am, they don't talk?" Birdie asked their mother.

"Ain't nothin' the matter with 'em but meanness," snapped Mrs. Slater.

Birdie took the little girls by the hand and led them out to the back porch. Here, her little brother, aged two, was playing in the water in the basin on the wash-shelf. A comb hung by a string from the porch post.

"What's that?" asked Essie, pointing.

"What—this? Why, a comb!" exclaimed Birdie. "Lemme comb out your hair."

"We ain't got us a comb, but Ma uses a shucks brush some-times," said Zephy.

The two little girls sat down on the top step. Birdie began to comb out their short, straggly hair. Combed smooth, it looked soft and pretty, curling up at the ends. In the bright sunshine, it shone like warm, glistening silver. Birdie brought the washbasin and washed their thin, pale faces. Their features were fine, their eyes blue as cornflowers.

"What's his name?" asked Essie, pointing to the little brother.

"Robert, but we call him Bunny," said Birdie. "We all got us

[10]

pet names. My big brother's name's Bihu, same as Pa, so we jest call him Buzz. My other brother's Daniel Alexander or jest plain Dan. My big sister's Dixie Lee Francine—we call her Dixie. My little sister's Dovey Eudora—we call her Dovey or Dove—she's asleep now. Me—I'm Berthenia Lou, but Pa calls me Birdie, 'cause he says I look like a little bird. Sometimes he calls me his little wren."

The lanky boy had ventured round the house and now stood staring.

"What's *your* name?" asked Birdie.

"Jefferson Davis Slater," he said gruffly.

"Purty good name," said Birdie.

"All but the Slater," said the boy, biting his lips.

Was he ashamed of his family? Birdie wondered. "What they call you—Jeff?"

"Naw. Shoestring—'count of I'm so long and thin. Never couldn't git no fat to my bones."

"Shoestring!" laughed Birdie. "That shore is a funny name!"

"Shore is!" agreed the boy, smiling. "I answer to Jeff, too."

Birdie took the mirror off the nail in the wall and held it in front of Essie. "See how purty you look!"

The little girls had never seen a mirror before.

"Oh!" they exclaimed. "Lemme see me in it!" They stuck out their tongues at their reflections and laughed.

Shoestring sat down. Birdie reached over and ran the comb through the boy's tousled black locks. Soon she encountered snarls. "Rats' nests!" she cried, jerking.

"Ow-w-w!" cried Shoestring, backing off. "Don't you dare rake me with that ere currycomb no more!"

The comb and mirror were not the only wonders. When Mrs. Boyer showed Mrs. Slater over the house, she exclaimed: "Sich fine fixin's you-all got!"

"They got a bed-kiver on their eatin' table, Ma," said Essie.

"Hit's a table-cloth," explained Birdie.

As Shoestring stared at the red and white checks, his face turned sullen. Then he burst out: "Guess oilcloth's good enough for anybody."

"I mean!" sniffed his mother.

[12]

Mrs. Boyer took down a pretty flowered plate from the shelf.
"Don't bother to show me no more of them fancy things,"
said Mrs. Slater, backing away. "Guess we seen enough of your
fine fixin's. Guess we know now how biggety you folks is, without seein' nothin' more."

"But, ma'am," begged Mrs. Boyer, "I didn't mean no offense."
The Slaters marched out through the breezeway without further words.

Mrs. Boyer quickly filled a cup with brown sugar and ran
after them. "Here's the sweetenin' you come to borrow, ma'am!"

But Mrs. Slater did not turn back or offer to take it. Down the
path she strode, her baby squalling and bouncing on her hip, as
she dragged the little girls along. Shoestring stalked behind, his
hands deep in his overall pockets.

"We got some right purty-lookin' plants," cried Birdie desper-
ately. She pulled off a geranium slip and ran after Mrs. Slater.
"Hit's a right purty pink, this geranium is, and Ma's got a Seven
Sisters rose . . ."

Mrs. Slater shoved the gate open. It had an old flatiron hanging on a chain for a weight. It closed behind them with a loud
bang. The Slaters plowed the sand with their bare feet and
vanished in the palmetto thicket.

Birdie went back to her mother, who was standing on the
porch. She looked at the cup of sugar in her mother's hand and
the geranium slip in her own.

"Reckon we can give 'em to her next time she comes," she
said.

CHAPTER II

Fences

"WHOA thar!" called Birdie. "Whoa, Semina!"

The white mule stopped. The girl thrust the plowshare into the ash-white soil again.

"Giddap, Semina!" The mule started on.

Again and again the mule had to stop. The soil was too light to hold the plow down, so she had to shove it in with vigorous thrusts.

The sun shone with merciless brightness. Birdie mopped her hot face under her sunbonnet. She started once more around the plot of ground with her plow. Her bare feet were black from the mucky sand.

Suddenly she noticed somebody hanging on the rail fence of the cowpen. It was the black-haired Slater boy. He had jumped off his horse and turned it loose to graze near by. She wondered if he would speak to her.

"Hey!" she called.

"Hey!" came the answer. "What you doin'?"

"I call myself plowin'," replied Birdie. "Wanna help?"

"Shucks—no!"

"Big ole lazy, you!" retorted the girl.

The white mule pushed on through the sandy soil. Birdie shoved the plow in deeper and watched the sand roll up in a high furrow. When she had made the round to the cowpen, she pulled up.

"What you plowin' for?" asked the boy.

"To grow things. Crops'll make mighty good here. This used to be part of the cowpen."

"Cowpen?" The boy looked blank.

"We been pennin' our cows up nights ever since we moved here," explained Birdie, "to git their manure scattered round."

"That what these rail fences is for?"

"Yes," said Birdie. "Pa fenced in this long lane first. Then he put fences across it to make pens. We got this whole piece manured that-a-way."

"You bring your cows up every night?" asked the boy.

"Shore do," said Birdie. "Ain't you seen me ridin' Pa's horse? But when we keep the calves penned up, the mother cows will come back at night of theirselves, so most of the time I don't need to bring 'em in."

The boy's face showed surprise. "Never heard o' no sich doin's as that. We let our cows run loose all year round. Don't bring 'em up but oncet a year. What you fixin' to plant?"

"Sweet 'taters, peanuts and sich. That's sugar cane over there," explained Birdie, pointing. "Pa and Buzz planted it when we first bought the place. It's doin' real well. We'll be grindin' cane shore 'nough, come fall. Right here we're fixin' to set strawberries."

"I mean! Strawberries!" Shoestring's eyes opened wide.

"Yes, strawberries!" said Birdie. "Heaps o' folks over round Galloway are growin' 'em to ship north. Pa heard a man called Galloway started it. So we're studyin' to raise us some and sell 'em."

"You purely can't!" said the boy. "Can't raise nothin' on this sorry ole piece o' land but a fuss!" He spat and frowned. "Sorriest you can find—either too wet or too dry. Not fitten for nothin' but palmetto roots. Your strawberries won't never make."

Birdie lifted her small chin defiantly.

[16]

❦❦❦❦❦❦❦❦❦❦❦❦❦❦❦❦❦❦❦❦❦❦❦❦❦❦❦

"Neighbors hung over Galloway's fence and said his'n wouldn't make, neither, but they did."

She turned the mule around and said giddap. "We're fixin' to plant corn and cowpeas between the rows," she called out. "Three crops offen one piece o' land!"

"Sorry-lookin' mule you got!" scoffed Shoestring. "She's windy—listen to her heave! Sounds like a big ole freight train chuggin'! Why don't you git a good horse like mine? Better'n ary mule."

Birdie glanced at the small, wiry animal which was nibbling grass behind him. Its hair was long and shaggy, as if it had never been touched by a currycomb.

"Pony, I call it," she said, with a sniff. "Little bitty ole sorry pony, no bigger'n a flea! Why, your legs are so long, your feet hit the ground as often as the pony's do!"

"He's a cowhorse," bragged Shoestring, "and I'm a cowman! This is my rope. I can catch ary thing I want to." He took the rope off the saddle and wound the loops carefully in his left hand. "You'd admire to watch me catch a steer. See that stump yonder? That's a wild steer. Be still, steer!" He swung the rope high over his head, then threw it, looping it round the stump.

"Huh! That's nothin'!" said Birdie. "Stumps don't move."

"Dog take it, I kin lasso your ole mule then!" boasted the boy. "Git her goin'!"

Birdie took up the lines and slapped the mule on the back. Semina began to move slowly along the row, pulling the plow.

"Grab that steer there, boy! Grab that steer!" yelled Shoestring. In a second he was over the rail fence, running through the sand. His rope went flying through the air.

"Don't catch me! Catch Semina!" Birdie dodged, but the rope hit her.

The boy pulled, and the loop tightened round her shoulders, throwing her down.

"I ain't a steer! You missed your aim!" She jumped up quickly.

Shoestring wound his rope and threw again. This time he lassoed the white mule, and stopped her in her tracks.

"See what a good cowman I am!" boasted the boy.

"Think you're smart, don't you?" replied Birdie. "Maybe you

can ride a cowhorse, but I bet you can't ride Semina!"

"Huh! That ole mule? She's half-dead already. Ary baby kin ride her."

"You jest try it," said Birdie.

The plowing done, she removed the harness and brought Semina out into the lane. Shoestring ran, threw himself over the mule's back, landed on Semina's ticklish spot and was promptly thrown headlong in the sand.

"Er-r-r-r, what'd your ole mule do that for?" sputtered the boy as he rose to his feet.

"She don't like cowmen," said Birdie. "They brag too much. And neither do I."

"Birdie!" called Mr. Boyer, entering the field. "What's a-goin' on out here? What you been doin' to that 'ere boy?"

"Semina throwed him, Pa!" said Birdie, laughing. "I was done plowing. That little ole shirttail boy got so biggety, I couldn't stand it no more."

Mr. Boyer was a tall, thin, genial-looking man, with a weathered complexion. He shoved his hat back and patted Birdie on the shoulder.

"Serves him dogged right!" he said, with a laugh. "Got rid o' him, eh?" He pointed his thumb after the retreating figures of boy and horse.

"Seems like them Slaters air hard folks to neighbor with," said Birdie, remembering Mrs. Slater's call. "Likely I had orter been nice to Shoestring; likely they won't come see us no more."

"They'll be back direckly; don't you pay no mind," said Mr. Boyer. "Tired out with all the plowin'? Little gal like you, no bigger'n a weensy wren, plowin' a hull big field like this!"

"I ain't no-ways tired," said Birdie, "but I'm so hot, I wisht I was a fish in the lake, swimmin' round nice and cool. When we gonna set the strawberry plants, Pa?"

"Right soon now," said Mr. Boyer. "I got 'em today. That's what kept me so long. Had a hard time findin' whar the ole man lives who sells 'em. Took the wrong turnin' in the piney-woods and losted myself and like to never got found again. The plants is beauties. Buzz and me'll git the sweet 'taters and peanuts planted tomorrow, and you and your Ma can start settin' strawberry plants."

"How soon do we pick?" asked Birdie excitedly.

"Pick! Don't count your biddies 'fore they're hatched, gal

[20]

young un!" Her father laughed. "You won't be pickin' no purty red berries till nigh a year from now. Soon as these plants git started growin', they'll send out runners enough to cover up the beds. In September, we take off the runners and set 'em out to make more plants. Then they stop runnin', and 'long about December, they begin bloomin' and . . . "

"Then we pick!" added Birdie, beaming.

"Yep! 'Bout next January we pick! But first, hit's a mighty hard job settin' all them plants."

Her father knew what he was talking about. Birdie agreed after the first day of setting. When she came into the house at suppertime, her knees and legs ached, her back ached, and all her muscles ached. She ate quickly and went to bed without a word.

Succeeding days saw the remainder of the plants set in neat double rows on high ridges in the fertilized land. Frequent rains gave them a good start, and the plants began to green up and stretch out fresh new leaves.

"I wisht that ere Shoestring could see how purty they air!" thought Birdie, filled with pride. "He said they wouldn't never make. I'd jest mightily like to show him."

But Shoestring did not come, nor any of the Slaters. Birdie often mentioned the fact, but her parents did not seem to let it worry them.

"They'll come direckly," said Mrs. Boyer. "Likely we'll see more of 'em than we want."

One day the boy passed. Birdie decided not to speak first. If he was still mad, he would go by without a word.

But he was friendly. He surprised her by handing her a big cooter—a soft-shell water turtle.

"Been fishin' over to Catfish Lake," he said agreeably. "Put me out a trout line, with white bacon for bait, and caught me ten cooters. Sold some of 'em, et some, and give some away. Tell your Ma to cook it. My Ma rolls 'em in flour and fries 'em in grease. Mighty good. Know how to clean 'em?"

"Pa does," said Birdie. "We like cooters when we can git 'em."

"My Pa's a great hunter," boasted Shoestring. "I like all kinds of meat they is—reckon I must be part Indian. I've et rabbit, frog, goat, possum, gopher, bear, deer, alligator and even rattlesnake!"

"Huh!" scoffed Birdie. "Bet you never ate no rattler. Bet it nigh choked you iffen you did."

"Tasted like chicken!" boasted the boy. "Alligator tastes like beefsteak, bear meat ain't much good, possum . . .

"I don't want no possum," said Birdie. "Hit don't appeal to my notion."

"Try cooter then," said Shoestring, and he was off.

After he left, Birdie wondered if he had nothing to do but go fishing all day. Then she remembered she had forgotten to show him the strawberry plants and tell him how nicely they were growing.

After the rains stopped, the strawberries didn't do so well. The plants began to dry up in the sun's terrific heat. Birdie carried water in a bucket and dipped it on them with a gourd dipper.

❦❦❦❦❦❦❦❦❦❦❦❦❦❦❦❦❦❦❦❦❦❦❦❦

She went out early every morning. But they continued to dry up, and more of them died.

"The strawberries don't make!" she wailed bitterly. "They're jest fixin' to die!"

One morning she saw a horse lying in the middle of the strawberry field. At first she thought it was dead. Beneath its shaggy coat, it was very lean and bony. She approached it warily. Suddenly the animal raised its head and looked at her. Then it began to roll. Over and over it went, its four feet pawing the air in awkward movements.

By the time it scrambled to its feet, Birdie had found a stick

and she gave chase. She flayed it with all her strength. The horse tore about aimlessly, tramping on rows where it had not wallowed.

"Mean little ole pony!" shouted Birdie. "You git outen here!"

Dan appeared, found a stick and began to chase too. Then Buzz and Mrs. Boyer came. They ran the horse off through the woods.

"Cowhorse!" cried Birdie in disgust. "That was Shoestring's cowhorse. He rounds up their cows with it."

When she went back to the strawberry field and saw the damage, she cried. Pa put his arm around her and said he would buy new plants to replace the others.

"We belong to build us a fence, Pa!" said Birdie. "Strawberries won't never make in an open field."

That same evening they found a bunch of cows with the S circle brand in the orange grove, pulling leaves and bark off the trees. Buzz discovered them while he was stripping Spanish moss off the topmost branches. He slid down and gave chase, whooping loudly. His shouts brought the rest of the family.

Off near the woods, Birdie found little Essie Slater. She had a stick in her hand and was whacking the back of a poor skinny beast, that kept on eating.

"Ole cow won't go home," wailed Essie.

The child's pale hair was more tousled than ever, and her face dirtier. She was the picture of distress. Birdie wiped off her tears, took her to the back porch and washed her face in the washbasin. Then she sent her home through the woods.

[24]

❧❧❧❧❧❧❧❧❧❧❧❧❧❧❧❧❧❧❧❧❧❧❧❧❧

Not till then did she notice that her young orange tree was nibbled off to the ground. She saw hoofprints in the soft earth where water had dripped from the pump. One of the Slater cows had gone home by way of the Boyers' backyard. It had stopped long enough to drink from the trough and eat up the fresh green leaves and branches of the young orange tree.

This time Birdie did not cry. She was too angry to cry.

"We belong to build us a fence," said Birdie. "We belong to fence in the grove and all the fields, Pa."

"You mighty right, gal," said Pa.

It was after the first rails had been split and laid along the outside edge of the strawberry field that Shoestring came along.

"How you like our new fence?" asked Birdie.

"Fence? What fence?"

Birdie pointed to the rails.

"What you fencin' for?" growled Shoestring.

"What we fencin' for? To keep the Slater hosses and cows out, that's what for!" Birdie's voice rose in shrill anger. "See what that mean little ole cowhorse o' yours done done? See whar he laid down in the middle of our strawberry field and wallered?"

Shoestring began to grin.

"What's funny?" demanded the girl.

"Wal—the bed was so sorry-lookin'," explained Shoestring, "nothin' wouldn't make there, the strawberry plants was all dried up to nothin'—even my ole cowhorse knowed it, so he jest thought it was a good place to waller in!"

[25]

Birdie glared.

"Think you're funny, don't you?"

"No," said Shoestring. His voice was serious. "I mean it. Strawberries won't never make there."

"Not less'n the neighbors keep their critters out," answered Birdie. "That's why we're fixin' to put up a fence. We're fencin' every acre of ground we own, every inch of field and woods and pasture. See them rails? They're gonna be a fence. Soon as Pa and Buzz git more split, there's gonna be more fence. Hear?"

"Yes," said the boy. When he spoke again, it was in a low, quiet voice. "I wisht you wouldn't fence. If there's ary thing my Pa hates, hit's a fence." He shook his head, frowning. "Ain't nothin' riles Pa more'n a fence."

Birdie stared at him. "Your Pa's got nary thing to do with it."

"Ain't he?" Shoestring looked at her earnestly. "I want to tell you somethin'. Do *your* Pa fence his fields in, *my* Pa will make trouble for him. I jest want you to know, that's all."

"What kind o' trouble?" asked Birdie in a scared voice.

"Can't never tell when it's Pa," Shoestring said slowly. "Pa's mean, and when he's drunk, you can't never tell what he'll do."

"He gits . . . drunk?" asked Birdie.

"Yes."

The boy turned and walked away. Birdie stared after him.

CHAPTER III

School

"IS it a fur piece?" asked Dovey.

"Not so powerful fur," answered Birdie.

She grasped Dovey's hand tightly and they hurried along. Dan came behind with the dinner bucket. Their path wound in and out through the scrub, around palmetto clumps, over trunks of fallen trees, under dwarf pines and oaks. The sand

was hard and hot under their feet, the sun still hotter on their heads.

They came to the flatwoods at last, where their feet made a soft patter on the pine-needle path. Innumerable tall straight trunks of giant pines rose up on all sides to join their tops in a green roof overhead. The sun made a pattern of light and shadow on the stubbly grass beneath. Here and there were cows grazing, or lying down, chewing their cud.

"Is it a fur piece?" asked Dovey again. "My legs is tired."

"We're most there now," said Birdie. "I hear young uns yellin'." In a moment, she added, "See! Thar 'tis!"

The schoolhouse was an old one, built of logs, with a stick-and-mud chimney at the end. On one side was the boys' baseball field. On the other, a rope swing dangled from a horizontal branch of a large live oak tree, hung with Spanish moss.

They came up slowly. A group of children playing by the door, stopped suddenly and looked.

"Let's go home," said Dovey, starting to cry.

"No," said Birdie. "We come to school and we're fixin' to stay." Dragging Dovey behind her, she approached the group. "Howdy!" she said.

They stared at her and she stared at them. One girl turned and spoke to the others. They all laughed.

"Howdy!" said Birdie again.

"You Yankees?" The girl, who had pale loose hair falling in her eyes, put the question. The other children crowded close behind her, their eyes cold with suspicion.

[28]

❦❦❦❦❦❦❦❦❦❦❦❦❦❦❦❦❦❦❦❦❦❦❦❦❦❦

"Shucks, no!" answered Birdie with a laugh. "We're shore 'nough Crackers! We was born in Marion County. We're jest the same as you-all." She put her arm round Dovey's shoulder. Dan said nothing.

"We don't want no Yankees in our school," said the girl.

Birdie looked at her. "I done tole you we ain't Yankees."

The girl looked at the others. "We heard tell 'at Yankees, with heaps of high-flyin' notions, was livin' in the ole Rodden-berry house. They come from up north somewheres."

"We come from Marion County, Florida—that's up north," said Birdie patiently. "We live in the Roddenberry house, but we ain't Yankees."

The girl seemed satisfied. "My name's Olema Dorsey. What's your'n?"

Birdie told her Dovey's and Dan's names and her own.

Olema began to be friendly. She pointed out the school children by name—Mary Jim Dorsey, Lank Tatum, Rofelia Marsh, Latrelle Tatum, Coy and Loy—the Marsh twins, the Hardens—Shad, Billie Sue and Roxie May—Kossie and Kessie Cook and others. They stood awkwardly and stared at the newcomers.

"What? No Slaters?" asked Birdie.

The minute she said it, she knew she had made a mistake. A frown went round the circle of child faces.

"Don't Essie and Zephy come to school?" she asked.

"Course not," said Rofelia Marsh. "They're little bitty screamin' young uns."

"How 'bout Shoestring, then?"

Rofelia Marsh looked at Olema Dorsey. "We don't mess up with no Slaters," she said.

What did this mean? Birdie was no wiser than before.

"Let's play ball," called Lank Tatum. The boys ran over to their side and Dan followed them.

"Want a drink?" asked Olema.

"Yes," said Birdie.

"Shore do," said Dovey.

They went to the pump. Olema pumped the water and her sister, Mary Jim, held the gourd. The children watched as Birdie and Dovey drank.

"Tastes of sulphur, don't hit?" said Birdie.

Nobody answered.

❦❦❦❦❦❦❦❦❦❦❦❦❦❦❦❦❦❦❦❦❦❦❦❦❦❦❦

"I wore my new calico dress," said Dovey.

As soon as she said it, Birdie wished she hadn't.

"Think you're biggety, don't you?" spoke up Billie Sue Harden.

Birdie looked around and saw that most of the girls' dresses were made from flour sacks. "No," she said quickly, "our dresses are calico, but not new. They been washed heaps o' times. See how faded they air?" They must not appear to be better than any of the others.

Billie Sue smiled. That made it all right. "Want to swing?" she asked.

"Yes," said Birdie.

"Shore do," said Dovey.

They walked over to the live oak tree.

"Your turn first," said Olema Dorsey.

Birdie swung and let Olema push her. It was nice to be a new girl in a new school and have the first turn. Next it was Dovey's turn, but while she was swinging, the bell rang. Birdie looked and saw a small, thin-looking man standing at the schoolhouse door.

"Is that . . . is he . . ." she began.

"That's Mr. Pearce, our teacher," said Rofelia. "He always makes us a talk of a mornin'."

The children crowded in, stamping their bare feet on the floor to shake the sand off. Olema took Birdie and Dovey to Mr. Pearce and told him their names. He gave them seats in the side row. It was nice to be a new girl in a new school and sit in the

[31]

side row by the open window. Birdie was happy. She knew she would soon like all the girls and they would like her.

School opened with a song.

Mr. Pearce stood in front with his back to the fireplace. A bamboo pole leaned in one corner, and a pile of fatwood, to burn on cold days, filled another. A small blackboard was on the rear wall. Mr. Pearce's voice was shrill, and all the children chimed in. When the song was over, Mr. Pearce made a talk and asked the children to be studious and to work hard to get an education.

The morning went by very fast. Dovey was put with the Marsh twins in the First Reader. Birdie was in the Fourth Grade with Olema Dorsey and Rofelia Marsh. Lank Tatum and Shad Harden were in the Fifth. Birdie wondered why the Slater boy was not there.

During recess they all played together as if they were old friends. At noon, Birdie and Dovey and Dan sat together under the live oak tree and ate their dinner. Other family groups were scattered here and there. Birdie opened the dinner bucket. It contained a bottle of cane syrup, pieces of fried rabbit and cooked hominy grits. They ate the grits with a spoon. They poured syrup from the bottle into the cover of the bucket and dipped their biscuits in it.

After they had eaten, the boys ran off to a bayhead a short distance away. A clump of trees grew in a low swampy place, near a pond. They tied a grapevine swing to the top of a tree, and hung onto it, to swing out over the pond. When the bell rang, they came back to their seats in the schoolhouse.

Lessons had already begun and Birdie was standing at the blackboard doing arithmetic when suddenly the outer door opened, and two large over-grown boys stumbled in. Mr. Pearce looked up at them over his glasses, but said nothing. The boys swaggered to their seats in the back of the room.

Birdie stared at them. The younger one reminded her of Jefferson Davis Slater.

When the teacher finished the lesson with the First Grade, he said severely: "Gus and Joe Slater, you were absent this morning. And tardy this evening. Have you a good excuse?"

"Yep!" said Gus. "We been rabbit-huntin'."

"Yep!" said Joe. "We been quail-trappin'."

"Seen a bunch o' wild turkeys," added Gus.

"Got too close and scared 'em away!" added Joe.

The children began to laugh.

"That will do!" said Mr. Pearce sternly. "Get out your books."

The Slater boys slammed their books on their desks. They shoved their feet out across the aisle.

Birdie went on with her arithmetic. So they were Slaters. They must be Shoestring's older brothers. She wondered why he was not in school. Maybe he was out rabbit-hunting too.

Mr. Pearce started the Third Grade spelling class. When little Latrelle Tatum went through the aisle to take her place on the recitation bench, she stumbled over Gus Slater's foot and fell.

Birdie ran, picked her up and dried her tears. She glared at the Slater boys. Did they come to school only to pester little children and make trouble?

"Have you no consideration even for a child?" Mr. Pearce's

[33]

voice was soft with reproach.

"Naw!" said Gus. "She don't belong to come round this way."

"We don't have to come to school, nohow," said Joe.

"Pa says he needs us to home," Gus went on.

"To hunt rabbits? To trap quail?" Mr. Pearce's voice was soft with sarcasm.

"Pa said we don't need to git book-larnin'," boasted Joe.

"Do you come to school," said Mr. Pearce gently, "you must study your books."

Gus and Joe threw their books on the floor in active defiance. "Jest try and make us!" they answered with a laugh.

Mr. Pearce picked up the bamboo rod and bravely walked to the back of the room. The eyes of all the children followed him. Some of the little girls began to cry. The room grew tense. Everybody knew something was going to happen.

Birdie slipped over into Dovey's seat and put her arm around her. She stared at the Slater boys, half-afraid and yet half-eager to see what they would do. She kept remembering they were Shoestring's brothers.

"You'll do as I say!" Mr. Pearce's voice was sharp, but it trembled. He raised the bamboo stick in the air.

The next moment Gus and Joe were on their feet, and nobody knew what was happening. The bamboo stick fell to the floor with a clatter, books and slates went flying through the air. The arms and legs of the two boys and the teacher became so mixed up, it was impossible to tell which was which. They rolled and tumbled over each other, and over seats, desks and floor.

[34]

❧❧❧❧❧❧❧❧❧❧❧❧❧❧❧❧❧❧❧❧❧❧❧❧❧❧❧❧❧❧❧

Shad Harden, who was twelve, took charge. Olema Dorsey and Rofelia Marsh were sobbing.

"Run outen here, everybody!" he called. He turned to Birdie. "Git the young uns out!"

With his help, she led the frightened, crying children out of the building. They huddled in a group under the live oak tree. They listened to the shouting and scuffling through the open door.

"Will they hurt Teacher?" the children asked.

"I hope not," said Birdie. "Teacher's a good fighter, too."

"They been studyin' to fight him for a long time," said Olema Dorsey.

"Now they done done it," said Rofelia Marsh, still sobbing in her handkerchief.

"Two agin one ain't fair." It was Lank Tatum who spoke.

"Let's go help Teacher," said Shad Harden.

Lank and Shad and several other boys ventured back in at the schoolhouse door. But they were too late. The fight was over. The Slater boys had finished their job. They came out the door and started off through the woods. They did not look at the children or speak to them. They had the air of being through with school forever.

Birdie shook her fist at them. She turned to the other girls. "I shore hope they never come back," she said.

"Shore do," said Olema and Rofelia.

They all shook their fists at the Slater boys' backs.

"We don't never want them Slaters in our school," said the

[35]

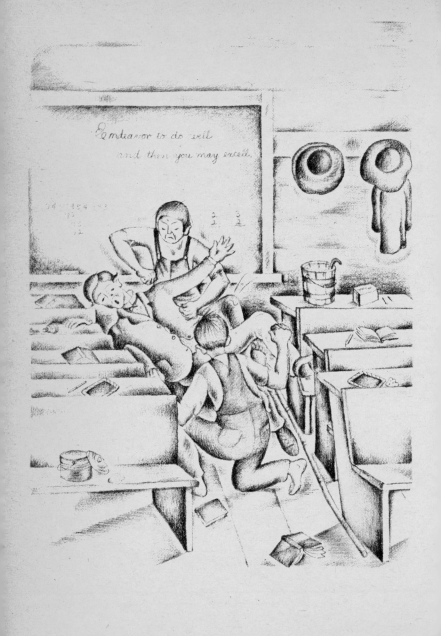

children. "We don't never want to see 'em again."

From the schoolhouse door, Lank Tatum beckoned to Birdie. Because she was the new girl, he beckoned to her, and not to any of the others.

"Tell the young uns to go on home," he said. "Tell 'em there won't be no school tomorrow. Teacher says so."

"Teacher?" gasped Birdie. "He ain't dead then?"

"He's beat up to a jelly," said Lank. "They shore whopped him good. Shad and me will git him home. We'll ride him on his horse and hold him so he won't fall off. Git the kids home first."

Birdie could just see the limp figure of Mr. Pearce stretched out on the floor. She went back to the children.

"Teacher says there won't be no school tomorrow," she announced. She felt sick inside with disappointment as she said it. She liked school. She liked being the new girl in a new school and having everybody be nice to her.

"No school tomorrow!" cried the children. "Goody! Goody!" They crowded round her.

"Is Teacher bad hurt?" asked Olema Dorsey.

"Did they beat the starch out of him?" asked Rofelia Marsh.

"All I know is he can talk," said Birdie. "He said no school tomorrow. We belong to go home now."

So they all went home. There was no school on the morrow, nor for many days and weeks thereafter, because the Slater boys had whipped the teacher. The first day of school for Birdie proved to be the last one for a long time.

[38]

CHAPTER IV

Hogses

"HOGSES!" shouted Pa. "Slater's hogses!"

Birdie sat up in bed and rubbed her eyes. It was the middle of the night, too dark to see anything. She heard the squealing of hogs, the scamper of sharp hoofs, and her father's voice yelling.

She jumped up and ran through the bedroom. A coal-oil lamp was burning on the dresser and she saw that the other beds were empty. She dashed through the kitchen, picked up a broom and went flying out the back door.

Pa's nightshirt flapped around his long bare legs, as he galloped over the white sand and waved the grubbing hoe in the air. Buzz had the ax, Ma had the rake, Dixie, Dovey and Dan all had lightwood sticks. They were chasing Slater's hogs. Only little Bunny had kept to his bed, sleeping through the excitement.

Like dark, swift-moving shadows, the hogs ran in circles over the strawberry field. They started in one direction, then turned off in another. They leaped and stumbled and sprang through the air, their long thin noses pointing the way for their skinny, long-legged bodies. The clamor of snorting and squealing was punctuated with the loud whacks and blows of the weapons laid on their backs.

After a while all the hogs were gone but one.

"Go back to bed, you-all!" ordered Pa. "I'm fixin' to deal with that feller myself!"

They hurried in, cleaned the sand off their feet and went to bed. As Birdie tried to go back to sleep, the grunts and squeals grew fainter and fainter. Then she heard one piercing squeal and a loud thud.

Had Pa killed the hog? Was there one hog less in Florida?

The hogs must have ruined the strawberries, but she forgot the damage in her concern over Slater's hog. She could not go to sleep until Pa came in. She heard him whispering to Ma and she wished she could hear what they were saying. She hoped he had not killed the hog. It would only make more trouble.

She must find out in the morning.

But when morning came, it was Sunday and nobody mentioned the hogs. They were busy getting ready to go to church. Today was the All-Day Sing and that meant taking dinner. Ma and Dixie worked hard packing the basket lunch. Birdie washed

❦❦❦❦❦❦❦❦❦❦❦❦❦❦❦❦❦❦❦❦❦❦❦❦❦❦❦❦

and dressed Dovey and Bunny, the boys fussed in front of the looking-glass, and soon they all climbed into the wagon and drove off. Dovey and Bunny sat on the seat with Ma and Pa. The others sat on slat-backed chairs placed in the wagon bed. They held onto the sides of the wagon as it jolted through the deep sandy ruts.

They were attending the Mt. Lebanon Church for the first time. It stood on a slight rise of ground which hardly deserved to be called a hill. The minute they got out of the wagon, the preacher came up and greeted the Boyer family. Other people came up and told their names. With all the welcoming, the Boyers soon felt quite at home.

The church was a long, boxlike structure, with two doors at the front gable end, and five windows in a row on each side wall. The inside walls and roof were ceiled with tiny narrow boards, varnished a dark brown. The pews were handmade benches with sloping backs. An organ stood in front, near the preacher's desk.

Dan and Buzz helped the boys pass out the *Old Sacred Harp* hymn books. First the people sang the notes, then words from the book. A pretty young woman with curly hair played the organ. As Birdie watched her fingers move over the keys, she forgot all about the hog chase of the night before. The organ music was rich and melodious. It was the nicest music she had ever heard.

Birdie saw Olema Dorsey and asked her who the organist was. Olema told her that her name was Miss Annie Laurie Dunnaway. She repeated the name to herself. It was almost as pretty as the

[41]

organ music.

The congregation kept singing all day long. Nobody had to sit through it all. People kept going in and coming out. They sat or stood and talked in the yard, then came in and sang till they were tired and went out again. They all did just as they pleased. It was a good time to visit friends and to make new ones. And the best thing about it was the organ music and the singing which kept on and on. Birdie talked to some of the girls she had met at school, and felt as if she had always known them.

At noonday, the preacher announced in a loud voice: "Dinner on the grounds!" and everybody was dismissed. In the piney woods behind the church were rough board tables, covered with table cloths. The women opened their baskets and spread out their rations, all the delicious dishes of the Florida backwoods. There was food for everybody—fried chicken, rabbit, squirrel, ham, sweet potatoes, cowpeas, grits and gravy, cakes and pies, corn bread and biscuit and plenty of cane syrup. Everybody ate heartily, laughed and joked, and talked in loud voices.

After dinner, the people strolled back into the church and sat down again. They waited for the organist to come and start the music. Birdie came to the door just as Miss Dunnaway appeared.

"Hit was mighty purty, ma'am . . . the music," she said.

"You like it?" asked the organist. "You play the organ too?"

"No ma'am," gulped Birdie. "Only . . . I'd like to."

"Maybe you will some day," said Miss Dunnaway.

"I . . ." Birdie could not speak.

[42]

"You are one of the Boyer girls? The new family in the old Roddenberry house?"

Birdie nodded. She wanted to say more, but the people were waiting. Miss Dunnaway hurried in. The music and singing began.

Birdie, left standing at the door, saw her father crossing the yard. Then she saw Gus and Joe Slater, and a man with them who must be their father. All thoughts of the organ music faded from her mind as she remembered the hogs. The man left Gus and Joe and came over to join Mr. Boyer.

Birdie slipped out around the corner of the church, where she could hear the men without being seen. She was trembling. She wished Pa had not chased Slater's hogs. Likely he was a good fighter like his sons.

[43]

It was the first time the two men had met, but they talked as if they knew each other. They sounded polite, not angry at all.

"I chased some hogs outen my strawberry field last night," said Boyer. "Might a been your'n."

"That so?" Slater looked up at him.

"Got a good fence, but it's mighty hard to make it hog-tight," Boyer went on.

"That so?" asked Slater.

"You know well as I do, them piney woods rooters can go under a gate and raise it off the hinges! They can turn a house over almost! Fence don't seem to do no good, keeping them out."

"That so?" repeated Slater.

"Of course you understand I don't want trouble with my neighbors," said Boyer.

"No?" said Slater.

"I'm a peaceable man," said Boyer, "but sometimes I lose my temper."

"Mighty glad to hear it!" said Slater, slapping him on the back. "I'm peaceable myself. Course we all know there's some matters that can only be settled with a shotgun!"

"There's the law," suggested Boyer.

"Wal—round here, a shotgun's more useful than the law, and handier, too!" Slater laughed.

"Speakin' of hogs," Boyer continued, "iffen you'd feed your'n, they'd stay at home and not bother other folks."

"Feed 'em!" cried Slater. "Why, man, they can find plenty to eat in the flatwoods—that's what them long noses is for. They

[44]

❦❦❦❦❦❦❦❦❦❦❦❦❦❦❦❦❦❦❦❦❦❦❦❦❦❦❦

eat snakes of all kinds, mice, rabbits, skunks and young foxes; acorns, palmetto buds and roots, and pine mast. And when they can't find none of them things, they can eat pine knots!'' He laughed at his joke.

''And the neighbor's corn and strawberries!'' added Boyer.

Slater laughed. ''I tell you what, Boyer, if ary hog of mine gets on your place, don't you hurt him, just take a switch and switch him. Switch him good.''

Boyer frowned, then he spoke slowly: ''I never kill other folkses' hogs or cows, unless I catch 'em on my place!''

''You'll never catch 'em! My razorbacks can run like a streak o' lightning!'' retorted Slater. ''They're regular wind-splitters. They can split the wind in two, they run so fast!''

Both men laughed heartily. They walked side by side and went into the church. They sat down on the men's side together and began to sing out of the same hymnbook.

Birdie had listened carefully and her fears were considerably relieved. Pa hadn't hurt Slater's hog after all. Pa knew how to handle Mr. Slater and keep him peaceable. Everything was all right again.

Birdie went in and began singing too.

During the afternoon, she strolled outdoors and joined a group of children gathered under the trees. Someone had seen a snake and the boys were trying to catch it. It slithered off under the palmetto bushes and they kept poking among the bristling, crackling leaves with sticks.

Essie and Zephy Slater were there, and several other children.

[45]

Shoestring boasted loudly that he would catch the snake alive.

"O-o-o-h, don't!" cried the girls, shuddering. "It might could be a rattler!"

"I'll catch it and whirl it by the tail till its head drops off!"

Birdie laughed. Still bragging, that boy!

Then she saw that he had caught the snake and was doing what he said. She watched the live snake go whirling through the air around his upraised arm. Horrified, she saw it slip from his grasp and come flying toward her.

"Shoestring! Don't you dare!" she gasped.

Then a blow struck her head which nearly knocked her hat off. She stood still, stunned. The other girls ran from her in fright. She wondered why they were running so fast.

❦❦❦❦❦❦❦❦❦❦❦❦❦❦❦❦❦❦❦❦❦❦❦❦❦❦❦❦

At first she did not realize what had happened. Then she saw Shoestring staring at her hat and she felt the unusual weight on it.

The snake was on her hat! On her Sunday hat!

She ducked her head with a sudden, violent motion. The snake fell to the ground and slipped off into the bushes. She saw that it was a young harmless blacksnake, but that did not change her feelings.

"You! You!" she yelled, shaking her fist at the boy.

She was so angry she wanted to kill him. She hated him with a cold hard hate. She hated his overalls and his black felt hat. She hated his thin face, tight mouth and half-shut eyes. She hated every bone in his skinny body. Her anger was black enough to kill him, but he ran so fast she could not catch him.

She came back to the church, went in and sat down beside her mother. She took her hat off and dropped it on the floor. She never wanted to see it or wear it again. She was trembling all over. She could not sing any more.

That night the hogs got into the strawberry field again. Birdie was awakened by the commotion, but she did not get up.

At breakfast, Pa said: "Reckon Slater will keep his hogs home from now on."

"Now, Bihu," said her mother, "we want to live peaceable, no matter how many strawberry plants they ruin."

"There's only one language some folks can understand," said Boyer, frowning.

Birdie looked from her father to her mother and wondered what they meant. Her brothers and sisters ran outdoors and paid no attention. All her fears returned. Were the Slaters going to spoil everything?

The second morning after the All-Day Sing she was sweeping the front porch when she noticed a piece of white tablet paper tacked up on the wall.

She saw there was pencil writing on it. With some difficulty she made out the words: *will git you yet jest you wate.* She read the words over several times.

Then she heard some one passing and saw it was Shoestring.

❧❧❧❧❧❧❧❧❧❧❧❧❧❧❧❧❧❧❧❧❧❧❧❧❧❧❧

She remembered the snake and she was still mad enough to kill the boy. Or, if she could not kill him, she would fight him. She clenched her fists behind her back. She resolved she would never speak to him again. Then she saw that he was dragging something along by a chain, something small and dark and furry.

"Nice little bitty puppy you got!" The words came out in spite of herself.

"Ha, ha! Hain't no dog! That's where you got fooled," laughed Shoestring. "Hit's a coon."

"Where'd you git it?"

"Out on the limb of a tree last night. My hound dog treed him," said the boy. "I can git me one ary time I want one."

"What you fixin' to do with it?"

"Gentle it. Keep it under the house to kill mice and rats," said Shoestring. "Make me a pen to keep it in. Learn it tricks. You want I should git you one?"

"No," said Birdie. She remembered how she hated him.

"Here, take this one," said the boy. "I kin git me another."

"Don't want no coon," said Birdie.

The boy hesitated, then pointed. Evidently he had brought the coon along for an excuse to cover his real purpose. He pointed to the paper tacked on the wall. "What's that 'ere paper stuck up there?" he inquired.

"Look and see for yourself," said Birdie.

"Can't read," said Shoestring.

"Good reason," said Birdie. " 'Cause you don't go to school,

[49]

that's why. Why don't you go to school, I want to know?"

The boy shrugged his shoulders. "Don't aim to mess up with no little ole school iffen I kin help it. What do the paper say?"

Birdie read it aloud: " '*will git you yet jest you wate.*' Who put it here?" she demanded.

"Haw! Don't you know?"

"Wouldn't ask iffen I did," said Birdie.

"You don't even know who put it there?"

"Your Pa, I reckon," said Birdie. "But why?"

"You don't know what your Pa done to my Pa's hog?"

Birdie's heart sank. He must have killed the hog, and it would only make further trouble. "Chased it outen the strawberry field is all," she said.

"Now don't you act so innocent!" said Shoestring. "You know well as I do he chopped the tips of our hog's ears off!"

"Huh!" said Birdie, with relief. The hog was not dead then. "Your Pa did it hisself. That's the way he marks 'em."

"No, it ain't!" said Shoestring. "Pa's hog mark is a round hole in the ear."

"Well, if my Pa done it, he meant it for a warning," said Birdie angrily. "He wants to let your Pa know that hog came on our place and did a heap of damage, and it better not come again!"

Shoestring pointed to the piece of paper. "There's my Pa's warning! Iffen your Pa don't leave our hogs alone, Pa means what he says: *he'll git him yet!* I jest come over to tell you."

Birdie looked the boy up and down.

[50]

❧❧❧❧❧❧❧❧❧❧❧❧❧❧❧❧❧❧❧❧❧❧❧❧❧❧❧❧❧

"So your Pa wrote this note and sneaked over here in the night and put it up, to say he'll get even!" Her voice was bitter with scorn.

"No, Gus done it," said the boy. "Gus learned to write at school."

Birdie looked at the note. "Iffen he'd stayed in school, he might a learned to write, you mean. But he whopped the teacher and broke up school. I was there, I know all about it."

"You do?" said Shoestring. "Well—he's too old to go now, he's sixteen."

"Iffen you went to school, you might could learn to write your Pa's notes for him, and sign your name to 'em. Whoever wrote this un didn't sign his name."

Birdie reached up for the paper and pulled it down. She folded it and tore it to bits. She threw the pieces on the porch and swept them angrily off onto the ground.

"Ain't your Pa seen it?" asked Shoestring.

"No," said Birdie, "and he ain't goin' to, 'cause it's tore up." She faced the boy boldly. "Hit's cowardly to write notes. Your Pa's scared to come and say what he's got to say to my Pa's face. Your Pa's a coward. Only cowards write notes and don't sign their names."

She expected Shoestring to get madder than ever when she called his Pa names, but he didn't. All he said was, "What we gonna do, so they don't git to shootin'?"

Birdie thought for a while. This was a surprise. It looked as if Shoestring didn't want trouble any more than she did.

[51]

He was trying to fix things up. All at once her black hate melted away and she liked him again. She was able to forgive him for the snake on her hat. She decided not to fight him for the snake. He only did it in fun anyhow. He had not meant to hurt or frighten her. Then she thought about the hogs again.

"You'll have to feed your hogs every night to keep 'em home," she suggested. "That's the onliest thing to do."

"But they're wild!" protested Shoestring. "They run wild and never come nigh the house, and that old boar, he's mean! Great-Grandpa was an old Indian fighter, and the boar cut him all to pieces last year, so he died."

Birdie had no time to think about Great-Grandpa Slater.

"Corn and peanuts and boiled sweet potatoes are good for feeding hogs," she said. "Hogs get tame soon enough if you feed 'em every night. Ours was perfectly wild once too. Now they're plumb gentle and come when I call. You jest try it."

"I got a better idea," said Shoestring. "I'll get my cowhorse and keep ridin' your fences every day, and whenever I see ary of our hogs come nigh it, I'll lasso him and take him home."

"That won't do. They come at night when you're in bed," said Birdie. "You got to throw 'em a mess of peanuts or chufers each evenin' to keep 'em comin' home. Hear?"

"I mean!" said Shoestring.

CHAPTER V

Overalls

BIRDIE was glad when it was her turn to go to town on Saturday. Dixie had to stay home to take care of Bunny and Dovey. Buzz and Dan had to get in wood. There had to be room in the wagon for the new cooking stove and the barbed wire, so only Birdie could go, besides Ma and Pa.

Like Ma, she was to have a new summer hat. She had never worn her old one after it had the snake on it. She put on her best dress and her long black stockings and high shoes. She knew she had to keep them on, no matter how hot it got. She fanned her hot face with her sunbonnet as they rode along. Pa said it was the hottest day they had had all summer.

Town seemed very far away because the road was new to her. It followed an endless sand-rut through miles of palmettos

[53]

in the scrub. Then it was a mere wagon-track winding this way
and that through the piney woods, and still farther along, it
became a corduroy road through a cypress swamp. When at
last they came to houses and began to pass people walking
on foot in the same direction, Birdie knew they would soon
be there.

They came to town, and it was filled with people because
it was Saturday. There was an open square in the middle, with
hitching posts under the trees. The depot, where the trains
came in, was on one side, and stores and houses on the other
three sides. The stores were mostly one-story buildings, with
wooden awnings jutting out over the sidewalks.

It was fine to be in town, to walk on board sidewalks instead
of loose sand, and to go straight into the millinery store.

"Howdy, Mis' Boyer! Howdy, Miss Birdie!"

Miss Liddy Evans stepped up to greet them. "Come right
in," she said. Although they were newcomers in the neighborhood, she knew them by sight and called them by name.

Miss Liddy was everybody's friend and no wonder. She
always had a smile or a joke or a laugh ready. She knew that
every woman, no matter how poor or plain, had a yearning
for pretty things, and she liked to please them. And she was
never too busy trimming hats or making dresses to help her
customers when they needed help.

Miss Liddy turned to a woman in the back of the store.

"Why, yes, ma'am, I shore will accommodate you," she said,
handing her some money. "You go right out and buy what you

[54]

need. And when your husband gets paid this evenin', you come pay me back. Now don't you worry a mite. Yes ma'am! Jest leave your baby right there on the couch in the back room. That's what it's for. There'll be plenty more there before the evenin's over, or I miss my guess."

The woman had a forlorn look, with her long, bedraggled skirts and stringy hair protruding from under her dark sun-bonnet. She slipped silently out the side door, clutching the borrowed money in her hand.

"Warn't that Mis' Slater, Ma?" whispered Birdie.

When Mrs. Boyer began to look at the hats on the stands, Miss Liddy came forward.

"A pretty straw for the little girl?" she suggested.

Soon Birdie was seated in front of a tilted mirror, trying on hats—hats with high crowns and low, wide brims and narrow, and with all kinds of fancy trimmings. Birdie thought they were all beautiful.

The sound of a baby's crying rang out.

"That's the Slater young un," said Miss Liddy. "Birdie, while I show your mother some hats, could you . . ."

"Yes-ma'am."

Birdie found the baby lying on a pile of quilts on a couch in the corner. Boxes, shelves, tables and chairs, a dressmaker's form and a sewing machine filled the back room. The floor was littered with snips and scraps of ribbons, laces, silks, cottons and fancy trimmings.

Birdie picked up the Slater baby and joggled it on her shoulder. She watched Miss Liddy's assistant trim a hat, lay it aside and take up another. It must be fun to trim hats.

Miss Liddy returned to the back room.

"Your Ma's takened the leghorn for you and a black straw with a feather for herself. She says for you to wait here till she comes back from the hardware store. Azuloy's fixin' to make some wax roses to take to church tomorrow. Would you like to help?"

"I'd be proud to, ma'am," said Birdie.

Azuloy, a fifteen-year-old orphan, was Miss Liddy's helper. She did everything from threading needles to sweeping floors. She had a table spread with tissue paper and wire, and a pot of paraffin melting on the little laundry stove.

[56]

Azuloy's blond hair was puffed up in front, and her single pigtail was tied at the back with a large black ribbon bow. Her face was thin, but her eyes were bright and eager. She wore a large white apron over her long full skirt.

"First you cut and shape the petals," she explained. "Then you twist paper around the wire stem and fasten the flower on the end."

They made pink and yellow and red roses. They dipped them in the melted wax. After they were dried, they looked like real ones, freshly picked from a living rosebush.

"Only they will never wilt," said Azuloy, smiling.

Birdie wished her new hat had a bright red rose on it instead of the black velvet band and streamers.

"They're for ornament," explained Azuloy, giving Birdie a bunch of the wax roses to take home with her. "Keep them in a vase on your parlor table. I can see you like pretty things as much as I do."

[57]

Birdie thanked her. Then the Slater baby began crying again. So did two others who had been brought in. Miss Liddy kept a supply of cold baked sweet potatoes handy. Birdie gave one to each of the babies and joggled them in turn on her shoulder.

A door from the millinery store opened into Wilkins' dry goods store beyond. Birdie glanced in and saw Jefferson Davis Slater, wearing his same old black felt hat and a clean suit of overalls, walking down the aisle. She called to him.

"Hey!" came the reply. "You in town too?"

"Yes," said Birdie. "Miss Liddy asked me to mind your Ma's baby." She walked into the dry goods store.

🌷🌷🌷🌷🌷🌷🌷🌷🌷🌷🌷🌷🌷🌷🌷🌷🌷🌷🌷🌷🌷🌷🌷🌷🌷

"Buyin' somethin'?" asked Shoestring.

"Ma and me's got us new summer hats," said Birdie.

Shoestring bit his lip. "I ain't never seed my Ma wear a hat on her head in all my life."

"And Pa's fixin' to git us a cookin' stove," Birdie went on.

"Cookin' stove!" snorted the boy. "Fireplace not good enough?"

"Ma gits tired bendin' over," said Birdie. "Pa promised her one, did we move to the Roddenberry place. And Pa's fixin to buy him barbed wire. Thought I'd tell you. He's studyin' to use it for fencin' stid of rails."

"Fencin'!" repeated the boy. He looked at her in silence.

"What you doin'?" asked Birdie, after a while.

"Buyin' overalls," said Shoestring.

"You shore need 'em," said Birdie, glancing at the ragged holes on his knees.

"Three new pairs," added the boy. He pointed to the garments spread out on the counter.

"You-all must be gittin' rich!" teased Birdie.

"Pa brung in a steer to the butcher," explained Shoestring. "I watched the butcher cut it up. Tough ole feller. Cow meat ain't fitten for nobody to eat. Hog meat's what makes you healthy! Give me a cup of gravy and some grits, ary time o' day, and I can make me a meal offen it."

"Did your Pa git paid for the steer?" asked Birdie.

"Not yet. He done tole Ma and Gus and Joe and me what he's gonna git for it and he tole us what we might could buy.

[59]

Then he went off to celebrate, he was feelin' so good." The boy bit his lip. After a while he added: "I got me three pair of new overalls anyhow."

"I'm proud," said Birdie. "Sorry too." The Slater baby on her shoulder began to whimper. "When's your Ma comin' back?"

"Dunno," said the boy. He reached for his package.

"Where's your money?" demanded the clerk.

"Pa will pay for it this evenin'," explained Shoestring. "Can't I take 'em now?"

"Not till they are paid for." The clerk put the package under the counter and turned his back.

Shoestring had no more than left the store when a loud commotion broke out. Dogs barked and howled, people screamed and ran.

"Dogses!" cried Miss Liddy. "Another dog fight! Can't get through a Saturday without a dog fight. Birdie, run fetch them two pails of water from the back room. I always keep 'em handy."

Birdie hurried and put the baby down on the couch. Pails in hand, she followed at Miss Liddy's heels, out the side door. Two dogs were at each other's throats, while a group of boys

pelted them with rotten oranges. Shoestring's hound was one of them, and he was trying to get hold of its collar, to pull it off.

"Stop chunkin' them oranges!" yelled Shoestring.

Miss Liddy took first one pail from Birdie's hands, then the other. With swift movements, she dashed the water into the dogs' faces. Surprised, they let go their hold, stopped their growling, and were easily parted. Shoestring wiped the water off his face, took his hound up in his arms and walked away.

"He might a said thank you," said Birdie.

"My!" said Miss Liddy, as they went back into the store. "The millinery business is shore lively—you got to lend money, tend babies, make wax flowers and stop dog fights!"

When Mrs. Boyer came back, it was time to eat. The Boyers took the dinner basket out of the wagon and ate on a bench in the square. Shoestring passed by, munching biscuit, his limping hound at his heels, but he did not glance their way.

A man brought a campstool and sat down near them. He opened a box and began to spread things out.

"What's he sellin'?" asked Ma.

"Safety-pins, likely," said Pa. "Horse trader was here last week. Peddlers often come too sellin' everything under the sun. Medicine shows, too, sometimes. They like the big crowd on Saturdays. Traveling preachers come on Sundays to preach."

The man set a canvas on a small easel, lifted a palette and began to paint with a long-handled brush. People strolled up to watch. Soon a crowd gathered.

"Can I go see?" asked Birdie.

"Shore can, young un," said Pa, smiling.

Birdie had never seen anything like it before. A landscape of green fields, trees and sky began to grow under the magic of the man's hand. Soon a road wound up the hill and disappeared on the horizon. Small specks of cows dotted a distant field. A flock of birds winged their way across the blue.

"See the Lightning Artist!" cried the man. He held up the picture which he had painted in ten minutes and said the price was three dollars. A man dug into his pants pocket for the money and took the wet painting away with him.

While the people looked on and admired, he began to paint a second landscape. Between strokes he unwrapped a whole gallery of other landscapes and sold them to bystanders.

"Sure money!" laughed Mr. Boyer. "Better than horse trading!"

"Ain't it wonderful!" cried Birdie. "Paintin' pictures fast as lightnin' is nicer than playin' the organ even!"

"Now, gal," said her mother, "don't you go gittin' silly notions in your head."

Shoestring Slater and his hound passed by again.

[62]

"Ain't he wonderful!" cried Birdie, pointing.

But the boy did not look up or listen. He strode past with his eyes fixed on the ground, his hands stuffed in his pockets.

"Where's your package?" called Birdie. "Your new overalls?"

He went on without speaking.

The afternoon passed all too quickly, and it was time to start for home. Birdie went with her father and mother to the hardware store and watched the men load the new stove and the rolls of barbed wire on the back of the wagon. The new stove was very black and shiny. On the oven door, in fancy letters, were the words Charter Oak.

It was when they came out of the store that they saw the Slaters. Mrs. Slater and her two little girls and Shoestring were huddled in a group, with the sad-looking hound dog at their feet. They were all crying but Shoestring.

Mrs. Slater dabbed at her eyes with the corner of her apron. She looked at the Boyers defiantly.

"Jeff said you-all was here buyin' a new cookin' stove!" she sniffed. "Gittin' more biggety than ever! Think you're better than other folkses, don't ye? And barbed wire! Fixin' to fence in your land, ain't ye?" Then she began to cry in earnest. "Whyn't you-all stay up there in Marion County where you come from? Why you gotta come down here and spoil everything?"

Birdie looked at Shoestring. The boy stood wretchedly by, leaning first on one foot then on the other. He didn't know what to do any more than Birdie did.

"What's the matter, Mis' Slater?" asked Mrs. Boyer kindly. "Can I do anything to help you?"

The next moment Mrs. Slater was in Mrs. Boyer's arms.

"Sam takened all the money he got from the steer and blew it in. He gambled most of it and got drunk with the rest," sobbed Mrs. Slater.

"Gus and Joe takened the horse and wagon and Pa in it and gone off," wailed Essie.

"We gotta walk home," added Zephy. "Such a fur piece."

"No, you don't," said Mr. Boyer. "You-all can ride with us. We can make room."

"I hate to be beholden to you," said Mrs. Slater, "but I'm shore obliged."

First Shoestring had to return all the purchases his mother had made that day, and collect the money. Then he went back to Miss Liddy's. Birdie walked with him. He handed Miss Liddy the money his mother had borrowed. Birdie got the Slater baby from the back room and carried it.

"Did your Pa get a good price for the steer?" asked Miss Liddy.

"Yes ma'am," said the boy.

"And your mother done got her all the things she needed?"

"No . . . yes ma'am!"

"And new overalls for you too, I hear."

"Yes ma'am."

Birdie looked at the holes in the knees of the boy's old ones, and understood how fierce was his pride. As they left the store, Miss Liddy's voice floated out after them:

"Tell your Ma to come again soon. . . ."

CHAPTER VI

The Storm

BIRDIE filled the gourd with cold water. She gulped it down but it did not seem to quench her thirst.

"Me thirsty too," said Bunny. "And me," said Dovey.

As she held the gourd for them, she sighed. Everything seemed to be going wrong somehow. Perhaps it was because it was so terribly hot. September was always the worst month, for it came at the end of the long, hot summer. After the September blows and rains, they would be able to breathe again. But day after day of sultry heat brought no rain.

Pa sent the children out to the field right after breakfast. The first thing they found was that something had been eating the vegetables. Something had torn down the stalks of corn and had stripped them of their ears. Coons? Gophers? The collard and turnip greens had been eaten. Gophers? Rabbits? Pa was cross when he saw all the damage. Even when you fenced against your neighbors' critters, there were plenty of wild ones to pester you, thought Birdie to herself.

Pa set the children to work in the strawberry field.

The strawberry plants which had lived through the summer heat had covered the ridges with runners. Pa said September was good setting weather. The runners had to be clipped off and re-set in the rows where the cowpeas and some of the corn had been taken out.

The old plants were left in place to grow strong for bearing fruit. They had to be weeded. Buzz had hoed them and left the weeding for the children. The grass and weeds around the plants had to be picked out by small fingers.

"You gotta goose-pick 'em," said Pa, "like geese eating grass —pull out every little ole grass blade you see."

Dovey, who was only six, soon got tired and kept begging for another drink.

"Ma said not to drink too much," cautioned Birdie. "It'll make you sick."

The heat was oppressive. It beat down upon the open field in waves. The sky was dark and lowering.

"Fixin' to rain soon," said Dovey. Her big eyes looked dark in her puny face. She had never been very strong.

"I mean!" replied Birdie. "Won't it feel good?"

"I'm fixin' to stay right out in the storm and get soaked to the skin," said Dan.

They begged for drinks again. So Birdie took them over to the well. It was simply a pipe coming up out of the ground, with a cap on the top. She lifted the cap and filled the gourd from the flowing stream.

"Hit's cold," said Dovey, smacking her thin lips.

"That's because there's a big underground lake right under us," said Dan. "I heard about a barn that fell right down in

[67]

a big hole and was never seen again. It was a sinkhole leading to the lake. If you dig a well big enough, the water will
spurt right up, high as the sky!"

Dovey opened her eyes wide.

"He means an artesian well," said Birdie. "Pa says we're
lucky to have six flowin' wells on the place. All he had to do
was drive pipes down in the sand, and the water came up of
itself."

"The Slaters got a sinkhole," said Dan, "but it goes dry in
hot weather. So they got to tote their water a fur piece."

The children went back to their weeding.

"Pa opened up all six of his wells and let the water run in
the strawberry rows to water 'em," said Birdie. "That's why
the berry plants never dried up."

"Wisht they had," said Dan. "Then we wouldn't have to
weed 'em."

"But jest think, next summer we'll have all the strawberry
jam we can eat," promised Birdie. The thought was a cheer-
ing one, but neither Dovey nor Dan responded.

"It's too hot out here," wailed Dovey.

"Up north, they got snow," said Birdie. "They make snow-
balls out of it and throw them."

"Wisht I might could see snow," said Dovey. "I'd eat some."

"Dixie might could come and help us," suggested Dan.

"Ma needs her in the house," said Birdie.

"My tooth's achin' again," said Dan. He began to cry.

" 'Count of that cold water you drank," said Birdie.

She left the two to their weeding and went to resetting the runners. She brought a pail of water to water them, and when she looked around, Dan was gone.

"He went that-a-way," said Dovey, "off in the scrub."

The scrub, that big wild stretch of dry and sandy land, where scrub oaks, scrub pines and palmettos grew, was an unexplored wilderness, always beckoning the children. Birdie could not blame him.

She worked awhile in silence. Then she noticed that Dovey was sitting in the row doing nothing. The child's face was very red under her checked sunbonnet and she looked sick. Birdie took her by the hand and hustled her to the house.

Mrs. Boyer had her sewing machine out in the breezeway, but she said it was hotter there than indoors. She told Birdie to sponge Dovey off with cool water and put her to bed. After that Birdie came out on the porch.

Suddenly she saw a great swarm of grasshoppers, three inches long, with red and yellow wings, settle down in the yard. Her amaryllis bulbs had come up nicely and had made a brave showing of gay bloom on both sides of the front path. In the early summer she had seen tiny black grasshoppers eating their leaves, but never as many as this. The grasshoppers had grown to maturity and they were devouring every lily leaf in sight.

Birdie forgot the heat. She took her long brush-broom and beat and whipped and swept grasshoppers. But she couldn't get rid of them. Another swarm came as soon as she stopped to rest.

[70]

"I can't kill all the grasshoppers in the world!" she wailed. They did not leave till all the leaves of her lilies were stripped. She sat down on the porch floor and cried.

"Hush up, honey!" scolded Ma, taking her foot off the pedal of the sewing machine. "Go find Bunny. I hear him crying."

Birdie walked round the house and found Bunny sitting in an ant hill, crying loudly. He was covered with ants. She shook and brushed him, then gave him a bath in the tin tub to get all the dirt off.

At dinner Pa scolded the children for leaving their weeding. When Ma announced that it was too hot to live, let alone work in the field, he said nothing more. He did not even inquire where Dan was.

After dinner, Ma had a headache and went in to lie down beside Dovey. Dixie got busy and scrubbed the kitchen floor with the cornhusk scrubbing broom. She set Bunny on it to hold it down, as she pushed it around by its long handle. Then Bunny fell off and got a bad bump. He cried long and loud, and Dixie had a hard time to quiet him.

Because so many things went wrong all day, Birdie was glad when she heard the boys' voices. Dan had come back and Shoe-

string was with him. All the dogs were barking. She went out on the porch.

"What you-all got?" she asked.

"Gophers! Fixin' to race 'em!" said Dan, his toothache forgotten.

Each boy carried a large gopher tortoise in his arms. They were enormous land turtles a foot across, with high, arching shells.

"Caught 'em in boxes," said Shoestring. "We found two gopher tunnels and set boxes in front of the holes, and they walked right in."

"Shoestring says they come out at twelve o'clock each day," said Dan.

"Don't believe it!" scoffed·Birdie. "How they know what time it is?"

The boys roared with laughter.

"Caught 'em anyhow!" bragged Shoestring.

"The dogs had a mind to tear the tunnels to pieces," Dan went on. "Thought they'd catch 'em some gopher snakes and rabbits and a skunk or two hidin' down in them holes."

"We'll race 'em," said Shoestring. "They'll race straight back to their holes, iffen they're young. If they're a hundred years old, they'll curl up under their shells and never move."

The boys put the gophers down on the ground on their backs. The animals began to pummel the air with their clubbed feet.

"One, two, three . . . GO!" shouted Shoestring.

❧❧❧❧❧❧❧❧❧❧❧❧❧❧❧❧❧❧❧❧❧❧❧❧❧

At the signal, each boy turned his gopher over, and they started out. The dogs pranced about and barked loudly.

"Come, have a ride, Birdie!" called Shoestring.

Birdie flew. She stepped on the back of a gopher and tried to ride. Dan stepped on the other's back. They hopped and slipped as the animals headed, with slow but steady speed, straight for the scrub.

"Pick him up and tote him back, Dan," called Shoestring.

The boys brought the gophers back and started the race all over again.

"I'm bettin' on yours."

A strange voice spoke. Birdie looked up and was surprised to see a strange man standing beside her. He had a ruddy, wrinkled face and frowzy hair. His ears stood out from his

head. His clothes were wrinkled and he carried a little black bag.

It was unusual to see a stranger. Not many people passed the house. Sometimes Negroes in wagons rode by on their way to the turpentine still farther north. Sometimes the Slaters or the Tatums or the Cooks passed on their way to town. But strangers were rare. Had the man dropped from the sky?

"Howdy!" said Birdie, remembering her manners.

People who passed were always invited into the house, but Ma was lying down with a headache. She stared at the man. She could not ask·him in, and she did not know what else to do with him.

The boys picked up their gophers and raced off. Birdie heard them say they were going to get ripe watermelons from the field, chill them in the rain-water barrel and eat them. They had not noticed the stranger.

"Doc Dayton's my name," said he. "Saw an alligator down the road a piece. Come out of the cypress swamp to cool off, I reckon."

Birdie smiled. She had seen plenty of alligators and knew all about them.

"Doc Dayton's my name," said the man. He repeated it a second time as if she had not heard. "Likely you don't know me. I'm the tooth dentist. I pull teeth of animals or humans, as the occasion requires. Any teeth need pullin' round here?"

"Oh!" exclaimed Birdie. "I'll call Pa," she started to run round the house, "and Dan."

She came dashing back at once. "How did you know Dan had the toothache?"

[74]

❦❦❦❦❦❦❦❦❦❦❦❦❦❦❦❦❦❦❦❦❦❦❦❦❦❦❦❦

"I can smell a toothache a mile off!" said the stranger.

Birdie smiled. Then she remembered her manners again.

"Won't you please set?" She waved her arm toward the rocking chair on the porch.

Birdie found her father in the field. Mr. Boyer was as glad as anybody to come in out of the heat. He brought Dan from the watermelon bed and the tooth dentist pulled Dan's tooth. Pa said Dan yelled loud enough to be heard all over Polk County. From the front porch they went to the barn.

"Could be Semina will stop being so ornery with those rotten teeth out," said Pa.

"Likely her teeth just need filing," said Doc Dayton. "Mules grind their food instead of chewing it. Their teeth git very sharp and need to be filed once a year by a mule dentist." He filed her teeth flat. "No more balkin' now. She'll be gentle as a cat right on."

Company, even passing strangers, always stayed for meals. The dentist stayed for supper and ate a big meal of vegetables in "pot likker," sweet potatoes, biscuit and syrup and watermelon. He told stories all evening. He made the Boyers almost forget how hot it was.

He needed no urging to spend the night. He decided to go to church with them in the morning. He said he might find some teeth to tend to, after the service was over. At any rate he would get a ride from there with somebody to the next town.

On Sunday it was so hot and close, it was like smothering to draw breath. Birdie fastened one of her red wax roses to the front of her new leghorn hat. She glanced in the looking-glass

on the back porch and smiled happily to herself.

When they walked into church, Miss Annie Laurie Dunn-away spoke to them. She said, "What a pretty hat!"

"When I get big, I'll have an organ and play like you," said Birdie.

The sky darkened. Birdie looked up and saw great flocks of birds all flying in the same direction. The air was very heavy.

It was on the way home that the storm broke. All through

[76]

the preaching and singing, thunder rolled and lightning flashed. When the wind began to blow, the preacher ended his remarks abruptly and dismissed. The people scurried to their wagons and buggies. Birdie did not see the tooth dentist again.

The wind blew. It blew all the hot, sultry air away. It blew fresh cool air in their faces. It blew great bunches of Spanish moss and dead branches of trees through the air. It blew the trees over until they nearly touched the ground. The trees bent low, straightened up, bent lower, straightened, and bent again.

Pa and Ma and the younger children crouched in a huddle on the wagon seat. The others threw the chairs down flat and lay down on their stomachs on the wagon bed.

"Don't raise your heads!" yelled Pa, as loud as he could above the roar of the wind. "Hold on tight!"

The wind tried to lift the frail wagon off the road and whirl it in the air. Osceola, the horse, bent his head and pulled hard. Suddenly Birdie's new hat flew up in the air and landed on a palmetto. Pa pulled up long enough for Dan to run get it. Birdie lay on top of it, and held onto the wagon sides with all her strength. Then the wind lifted one of the chairs and it went whirling off, but they did not stop again. They came to a large pine tree, blown down across the road, and Pa had to drive around it.

Pretty soon the rain came. Like sharp pebbles, it bit into their skin. It pounded their bodies without mercy.

When they got home, they saw that the roof of the chicken house had been blown off and was leaning against the barn. The yard around the house was a great puddle. They did not stop to see what further damage had been done. They ran for the house, where they closed all the wooden shutters and braced all the doors.

Indoors, Birdie looked at her new hat. The rain had washed all the color out of the paper rose and had stained the straw a bright pink. The crown was mashed flat.

"You're a sorry sight," said Birdie. She put it down with a sigh.

Then she drew a deep breath. The hot spell was over.

CHAPTER VII

Cane Grinding

GIDDAP, Semina! Giddap!"
The white mule was hitched to the end of the long sweep. Birdie hit her over the back with a stick. She hoped she would not balk today.

Summer was over and cane grinding time had come. The sweet potatoes had been dug in August and stored in layers of pine straw on the floor of the potato house. Fodder and corn had been stowed away in the crib, along with dried peanuts and chufers—winter feed for the stock. Hogs had been butchered, hams and sides of bacon smoked, and sausage made.

The cane crop was good. Pa said it would take two or three weeks to grind it all. There would be syrup to sell, and plenty of brown sugar and molasses to eat all year.

"Git that lazy ole mule goin'!" yelled Buzz.

Birdie whacked Semina as hard as she could.

The cane mill had two iron rollers set vertically on a pine framework, and a long, curved pine-trunk sweep fastened on top. The mule was hitched to its lower end, while the short upper end swung free as a balance. Buzz stood under the sweep and fed sugar cane into the slowly grinding rollers.

"Git her goin'!" yelled Buzz.

Birdie whacked the mule again.

Semina moved slowly. Round and round the cane mill she walked in an endless circle. The rollers, though well-greased with tallow, began a loud screak, scre-ak, scre--ak, which could be heard far and wide.

Mr. Boyer had sent word to all the neighbors that he was grinding cane. People began to drop in—the Tatums, the Cooks and others. The men went to the field where they cut the long cane stalks and hauled them in. They took turns feeding the stalks into the rollers. Cane pulp, called "pummy" fell to the ground at one side.

🌷🌷🌷🌷🌷🌷🌷🌷🌷🌷🌷🌷🌷🌷🌷🌷🌷🌷🌷🌷🌷🌷🌷

The pale green milky-looking cane juice poured out slowly into a barrel on the other side. Flies began to come, attracted by its sweetness. Like the flies, children and grown-ups came too, all eager to taste.

"I always put on ten pounds in grinding season," said Mrs. Tatum, a plump young woman with a hearty laugh.

She dipped a tin cup into the sudsy liquor and drained it dry. She filled it again for Lank, her son, and Latrelle, her daughter. Other children crowded close, eager for drinks.

"Hit looks like ole dirty, soapy wash-water to me," said Shoestring Slater, frowning.

"But hit tastes sweet like sugar candy to me!" retorted Birdie.

"Hey! Don't drink too much!" cried Mr. Boyer. "Or they won't be none left for your candy-pullin' this evenin'!"

"Candy pullin'! Candy pullin'!" The children danced with excitement.

"Yard-plays! We'll have yard-plays too!" they cried.

When she was sure that Semina was going in good form, Birdie ran back to the house. Already it was full of people. The Hardens and the Dorseys had come. The Marshes with Rofelia and the twins, Coy and Loy, were there. And Mrs. Slater with her baby and Essie and Zephy.

"Git out and play with the other young uns!" ordered Mrs. Slater. "Can't have you underfoot all day."

But the little girls were shy and refused to move.

"Come with me," said Birdie, smiling.

Birdie could not help thinking about the hog with its ears cut off, and the note on the porch. It seemed strange that the Slaters, who were the Boyers' worst enemies, should act like good friends and come to the cane grinding. But quarrels did not keep people away from frolics, she knew that. It was an unwritten law of the backwoods.

She found Dovey and took the three little girls to a shady spot under the big umbrella tree. She made play dollies out of towels for them. She brought sugar cane, peeled it down and gave them pieces to suck and chew. She promised them candy at the candy-pulling in the evening.

With a piece of sugar cane in her mouth, she ran back to the mill. Semina was still making her obedient rounds. The mule walked with her eyes closed as if she could go on forever. There was no need to whack her.

🌷🌷🌷🌷🌷🌷🌷🌷🌷🌷🌷🌷🌷🌷🌷🌷🌷🌷🌷🌷🌷🌷🌷🌷🌷🌷🌷

Two barrels had been filled with cane juice, and the syrup-making had begun. Under the roof shelter near by, a big sixty-gallon kettle of the green liquid was bubbling away on top of the brick furnace. Shoestring, Lank and other boys brought up armfuls of pine wood to feed the fire, which glowed red from the open end and sent clouds of black smoke up the tall chimney.

Mrs. Tatum, very red in the face, had charge of the syrup-boiling. She stirred it constantly with a long-handled dipper to keep it from boiling over. Now and then she skimmed it, dipping the green foam off into a barrel at one side. This was saved, and when fermented, would be made into a sweetish-sour beer.

Gradually, the cane juice changed from green to a warm

yellowish color with flecks of red. When bubbles appeared at the top, it was done. A cedar trough had been put up on blocks. Mrs. Tatum dipped the syrup out of the kettle into the trough, to allow it to cool.

Birdie and Shoestring and Olema Dorsey and Lank Tatum made little paddles of cane, and began to scrape off the fine scum rising on the surface of the syrup, and eat it with relish. Sweet potatoes, tucked under the edge of the syrup kettle, had baked quickly, and now found their way into the children's hands.

The men refilled the kettle on the furnace with fresh cane juice for the next boiling. Mrs. Tatum went into the kitchen and Mrs. Dorsey came out to take her place.

It was when the grinding and boiling were at their height that Semina took it into her head to balk. She stopped in her tracks and refused to move another step. Mr. Dorsey beat her with a stick, but she did not appear to feel it.

The feeding of the cane stopped. No more juice poured into the trough. The kettle on the furnace was empty. Everything stopped because of Semina.

Birdie stepped up. "Likely I can get her started."

She tried everything.

She whispered in her ear. She whacked her on the back. She tickled her ticklish spot. She held brown sugar in her hand to tempt her sweet tooth. She offered her a chew of sugar cane. But the white mule turned away with cool indifference.

"Honey," said Pa, "you can't do nothing with her."

The men stood around and laughed at Birdie. She got red in the face and redder. At last she spoke to Pa.

"Likely her teeth need filing again," said Birdie. "The tooth dentist said that would stop her from balking!"

The men roared with laughter. Embarrassed, Birdie fled. She took refuge behind the big umbrella tree. Then she heard the rollers creak again, and saw that somebody's horse had been put in Semina's place. The cane grinding went on.

At dusk-dark the real fun began.

Sam Slater and Gus and Joe appeared. No frolic was complete without them. Sam brought his fiddle into the house and struck up a lively tune, while Shoestring stood at his side and picked on the violin strings with knitting needles, for an accompaniment. The men and women formed into lines and Sam Slater called the dance steps in a loud voice. Soon the rooms and porches were a flurry of movement, music and laughter. Joe Slater danced fancy steps, and made the people laugh. "He shore can cut the fool!" they said.

Outdoors, the children and young people began their yard-plays. Gus Slater played his mouth organ with gay abandon. They took partners, formed a circle and sang:

> "How happy was the miller when he lived by himself,
> The wheel rolls round and he gathers in his wealth;
> One hand in the hopper and the other in the sack,
> The wheel rolls round and he hollers out *grab*!"

Whereupon each boy grabbed the girl in front of him, and kept on whirling. Gus Slater happened to be next to Birdie. He

[85]

caught her up and swung her so high, her feet did not touch the ground till she got round the circle.

"You put me down, Gus Slater!" she cried indignantly.

They played and sang *Get on Girls and Go to Boston*. After that came *King William was King Joseph's Son, Go Forth and Face Your Lover* and *Green Grows the Willow Tree*. They played the games until their voices were hoarse and they were ready to drop.

Meanwhile Mr. Boyer had set fire to a pine stump near by. When darkness came down, he had a great bonfire burning to light up the yard. The boys ran to pile on more lightwood knots whenever it burned low. It hissed and crackled and popped, bathing the dancing figures in a pattern of light and shadow.

Mr. Boyer made the candy himself. He boiled the syrup down to just the right temperature, then poured the thickening mixture out on many plates to cool. A brisk rush followed, as each boy hurried to get a plate for his girl.

Birdie took plates to the little Slater girls and Dovey and showed them how to pull. By the time she got back, most of the boys and girls had teamed up. Shad Harden was pulling candy with Olema Dorsey, and Lank Tatum with Rofelia Marsh. She stood around for a while, wondering who would pull with her.

She hoped it would not be Shoestring Slater. She was getting sick of the Slaters.

But she could not get away from him. He stood in front of her and blocked her path. For once he was not wearing the black felt hat. He held out a plate of candy. He smiled shyly, but did not look happy.

[86]

"Know how to pull?" he asked.

"Shore do," she said.

They greased their hands. Shoestring clamped his hands on the ball of candy and they began to pull. The candy swung back and forth, growing lighter and paler in color and gradually hardening. Shoestring's hands were big and strong for pulling, but he said not a word.

All the boys and girls were laughing and screaming. Some got candy in their hair and had fun taking it out. Birdie wished she were with someone else. She watched Lank Tatum and Shad Harden. They liked fun, they knew how to laugh. Olema and Rofelia were having a fine time.

[87]

But Shoestring was as glum as if he were at a funeral.

"I got somethin' to tell you," he whispered.

Birdie looked at him.

His eyes were sullen. His lips were closed in a hard thin line. Couldn't he laugh a little even at a frolic? If he couldn't laugh, he might could stay home. Why, there was always more fun at candy-pullings than at anything else. Why did he have to spoil everything?

"Trouble again," said Shoestring, mysteriously.

Birdie was sick of the word, but she said nothing.

Shoestring took out his knife and cut the hardened candy into pieces. They held the plateful between them as they stood under the umbrella tree. The little girls' play dollies were lying there on the bench.

"What is it?" asked Birdie.

Shoestring offered her candy, and she put a piece in her mouth.

"Pa knows about your new barbed-wire fence," said he.

"What of it?"

"Our ponds got all dried up from the dry summer," explained the boy, "so this morning Pa told me to drive the cows over to Catfish Lake for water. I got on my cowhorse and . . ."

"Then what?" asked Birdie.

He offered her candy, but she couldn't eat any more.

"I come right back. I tole Pa: 'Boyer's done fenced in the right o' way to the lake'."

"Pa and Buzz been so busy all summer," said Birdie, "they

[88]

❧❧❧❧❧❧❧❧❧❧❧❧❧❧❧❧❧❧❧❧❧❧❧❧❧❧❧❧❧❧

jest got round to puttin' the fence up last week. What'd you tell him for?"

"Had to. He'd a found it out for himself," said Shoestring.

"What's he fixin' to do?"

"Make trouble."

"But he come to our cane grindin' and he's in the house right now callin' all the dances," cried Birdie in protest. "He don't mean us no harm."

"Don't he!" The boy spoke scornfully.

"How you know?"

Shoestring hesitated, looking at her hard. Then he said, "He's got the pliers in his pocket."

CHAPTER VIII

Cattle

"I JEST knew he would!" said Pa. He spat in the sand.

"What you fixin' to do, Pa?" asked Birdie.

Mr. Boyer put his hand under her chin and tilted up her bird-like face. "Sugar," he said softly, "don't you git worried now."

"You won't make a ruckus, Pa?" she asked. "Ma says you jest love to make a ruckus."

"Sugar, I'm studyin' what's best to do," said Pa. "Of one thing I'm certain. When there's trouble waitin' for you, you jest as good go out to meet it."

It was the morning after the cane grinding. Birdie had found tracks of cattle running straight through the strawberry field, across the pasture and on down to the lake. The new wire fence had been deliberately cut to let the cattle through.

Her father looked at the trampled strawberries and the mangled fence.

"He ain't forgot, after all!" he said.

Birdie had not believed Slater would do it, even when Shoestring told her about the pliers. That time, in early summer, when Pa Boyer had marked the hog's ears, as a warning to Slater, nothing had happened except the note on the porch, which she herself tore to bits.

After that, the hogs had not come so often. She wondered if Shoestring fed them every night and if regular feeding had kept them home. He never told her, and she had never asked him. Some way, she didn't like to bring the subject up.

It was better, as Pa said, to let sleeping hogs lie. Time enough, when they woke, to deal with them. This looked like the time. Slater had not forgotten. He was getting even.

Pa was as determined as ever to get his farm fenced. Through the fall, he and Buzz had been using their spare time to stretch barbed wire on all their outer boundaries. Now it was cut to bits. All four wires were cut between every post for the distance of a quarter of a mile.

Pa just stood and looked at it. He didn't say another word. He didn't do anything about it. He didn't go near the Slaters or call them to account. He didn't even mention the Slaters by name.

The next Saturday he took a lot of cane syrup to town to sell. He said he wanted to buy white paint to paint the house.

"You mean you want to get more barbed wire," said Ma.

"You shore do love a ruckus. Why don't you let the fence go, and live peaceable?"

Pa ignored her question. "I'm studyin' to paint the house, come spring. I want to buy the paint now, when I can pay for it."

Ma stayed at home to hoe up the trampled strawberry plants.

Birdie and Dovey went along to town with Pa and Buzz. Birdie took her leghorn hat to Miss Liddy's, the way Ma told her to. Azuloy worked on it most of the afternoon, while the girls watched. She bleached it, reshaped and retrimmed it. When it was all done, it had a beautiful red rose on it. This one was made of silk, not paper. The hat looked as good as new.

Birdie and Dovey waited at Miss Liddy's while Pa took care of his business. It took him a long time. They thought he would never come. They watched for him at the front window. Miss Liddy gave them cold boiled sweet potatoes to eat, to keep them from getting hungry.

The Tatums passed, and other people they knew, but Pa did

🌷🌷🌷🌷🌷🌷🌷🌷🌷🌷🌷🌷🌷🌷🌷🌷🌷🌷🌷🌷🌷🌷🌷🌷

not come. Suddenly a loud, shuffling noise filled the air, a rumble made by the tramping of sharp hoofs, and the mooing of cattle. Above the commotion, loud shouts rang out.

"What's that? Shootin'?" asked Birdie.

"Oh, I'm scared!" wailed Dovey.

Miss Liddy hurried over. "The Crackers are coming," she explained. "Just cowmen with their cattle! Hear how they crack their long, rawhide whips. They're driving a big herd to market at Tampa, to ship to Cuba most likely. Probably came from way up yonder by Jacksonville, buyin' up beef cattle all along the way." She paused. "Folks born in Florida or who have lived here a long time are called Crackers—after the cowmen."

"We're Crackers!" said Birdie proudly. "We was born in Marion County!"

For half an hour, the air was filled with horseflies and gritty dust; the clay-packed street was ground to dry powder by sharp hoofs. The cowmen rode small, wiry cowhorses, and cracked their whips beside the herd, shouting and whooping and singing lustily:

> "Sittin' on a cowhorse
> The whole day long,
> Thinkin' of those good times,
> All past and gone.
>
> Apple like a cherry,
> Cherry like a rose;
> Oh, how I love my Cindy
> Nobody livin' knows!"

An oxcart brought up the rear, carrying supplies. The teamster, who also served as cook, walked to the left of the cart, swinging his whip back over his shoulder, then whipping it forward in a startling crack, that sounded like a shot from a gun.

The great stream of cattle passed slowly out on the rutty Tampa road. The dust settled down and the town was left to its usual quiet.

When it was time for Miss Liddy to go home for supper, she said, "I must buy those schoolbooks for the Harden children—they're coming in to town to school; they live near enough. Their Pa asked me to. We'll go down the street and keep an eye out for your father."

Miss Liddy bought the books at the drug store, then they walked round the block. It was supper time and there were few people about. The square was deserted. A mule, pulling a rickety wagon, went by. An old woman on the seat had a little bell which she rang now and then.

"That's old Janey Pokes sellin' vegetables," said Miss Liddy.

"When I start sellin' strawberries," said Birdie, "I'll get me a wagon and a bell."

"You'll be a strawberry girl, won't you?" said Miss Liddy.

When they passed by the saloon on the other side of the street, they heard a loud commotion inside. The double half-screen which covered the open front door swayed back and forth. Men's legs could be seen beneath it, kicking and fighting in lively fashion. Loud voices were shouting.

"Come away!" cried Miss Liddy. "Such wicked men, in such a wicked place! They've been drinking!"

[94]

She pulled the two girls after her.

"But I heard Pa!" protested Birdie. "I'm sure it was Pa!"

"Why Birdie!" said Miss Liddy. "I hope your father never goes in *there*!"

"He's in there now," said Birdie, pointing. "I can tell him by his overalls. That's the patch Ma put on yesterday." The overalls in question were still kicking briskly.

Miss Liddy was struck dumb with astonishment.

"Can't I go in and tell him we want to go home?" asked Birdie.

"I should say *not*!" Miss Liddy put her arms around the girls. The shouting of the men continued. While they waited, they could not help but hear what the men were saying.

"You've no right to cut my fence!" shouted Mr. Boyer.

"You've no right to cut off my right o' way!" answered Slater. "We've always lived there, me and my Pa and my Grandpa before me! Grandpa was an old Indian fighter and he come there right after the Seminole War! We've always had the use of all that land for pasture, for moss pickin' and frog huntin' and anything else we want. You got no right to fence it up!"

"I'll fence in what I paid for!" shouted Mr. Boyer defiantly. "What's mine's my own! I'll fence it in and keep other folks and their stock out!"

"Ary time you fence off the right o' way to the lake, so my cows can't get to water, I'll cut your fence!" Slater's voice was shrill with anger. "See, I got my pliers right here!"

"Better not try it again!" warned Boyer. "I'm allowed to shoot a man if he enters my house or bothers my property! If I catch anybody on my property that I paid good money for, I'll shoot! Did you pay money for your land?"

"No . . ." admitted Slater. "We done always lived there since Grandpappy's days."

"You're a squatter! You don't own an inch of land and yet you got three hundred head of cattle to pasture out on other people's property! You don't even own the land your house is settin' on, do you?"

"Wal—not exactly . . . but what difference do that make?" cried Slater. "Hit's Open Range! Everybody knows that! Everybody leaves their stock run loose!"

"Not across my place they don't!" said Boyer in a quiet tone.

[96]

❦❦❦❦❦❦❦❦❦❦❦❦❦❦❦❦❦❦❦❦❦❦❦❦❦❦

"I warned you before: if I catch a cow or a hog of your'n on my place, I'll shoot on sight! Open Range—we'll see! We'll get a Fence Law passed!"

"A No-Fence Law, you mean!" yelled Slater.

Other men chimed in. "That question won't never be settled till doomsday!" they said.

"Fence cutting!" cried Miss Liddy, standing outside on the plank sidewalk. "So that's it! Nothin' like fence cuttin' for causin' trouble. Florida won't never be a peaceable place to live till that question gets settled. But such talk is not fitten for you children to hear. Come, I'll take you home with me. You can sleep to my house."

But Birdie and Dovey refused to go.

"Pa-a-a! Pa-a-a!" Dovey began to cry. "Pa-a-a!"

"We'd jest as soon wait here till Pa comes out," said Birdie, with spirit. "Pa can beat the starch out of Slater, I reckon! He'll take us home, soon as he gits done."

"You don't think he might be . . . drinking?" asked Miss Liddy.

"No ma'am," said Birdie. "He's not drunk, if that's what you mean. He don't drink. He just came here to find Mr. Slater and give him a talkin'-to, 'cause he cut our fence."

Miss Liddy had to hurry home to supper, so she could get back to the millinery store for the Saturday night trade. After she left, Birdie and Dovey waited a long time. Things quieted down inside the saloon. After a while Slater left, looking feeble and battered, with a man on each side holding him up. Then

Mr. Boyer came out alone. He looked quite unharmed.

The girls ran to him and took him by the hand.

They went to the wagon, but Buzz was not there. Pa had bought barbed wire and white paint both. He loaded them on. They waited till Buzz came. He had a black eye, and said he had had a fight with Gus Slater. Pa grinned.

"But he got worse than I did," added Buzz. *"He's* in jail."

It was night when they got home. Ma reported that the Slater herd had gone through the strawberry field again on their way to the lake. Shoestring had driven them.

Pa unloaded the wagon. Ma did not say a word about the white paint.

"I see you got more wire," she said.

Then she scolded Pa and Buzz for fighting the Slaters.

"Fighting don't settle anything. There's more peaceable ways to handle this . . ."

"Now jest what," asked Pa, with sarcasm in his voice, "would *you* do?"

"I'll show you!" said Ma with spirit. "Next time he comes to cut that fence, I'll get him to turn round and leave it uncut. And I won't say a word to him neither."

Birdie opened her eyes wide. Could Ma handle Slater better than Pa and keep things peaceable?

The following week Mr. Boyer lost no time in putting the new fence up. Mrs. Boyer expected something to happen. She told the children to keep a sharp lookout and to let her know if any of the Slaters appeared—or any of the Slaters' cows or hogs. She did not have to wait long.

One day toward the end of the week, Dovey and Dan came running in. "The Slaters are comin'!" they called. "They're drivin' their cattle this-a-way!"

Pa was off on the other side of the farm, but Ma was ready. She told the little children to stay in the house with Dixie. Armed with flour sacks, she and Birdie hurried out to the strawberry field. They sprinkled flour on the strawberry plants in the rows next to the wire fence.

The herd of woods cattle came closer and closer, on through the scrub. They were small, thin and wiry, with protruding hip bones and long horns. They had grown runty from foraging for tough wire grass, from traveling through saw palmetto thickets, sidestepping rattlesnakes, jumping over gopher holes, and withstanding heat, rain, flies and mosquitoes.

The cattle came up to the fence and stopped. They massed in a confused huddle.

Shoestring, riding his cowhorse, pushed his way through the herd. His father, on another horse, made his way up from behind. They had expected to drive the cows right through, but the new fence was in the way.

"Got your pliers, Pa?" called Shoestring. He shouted in a loud bragging tone, so Birdie could hear.

"There ain't no fence can stop me!" called Slater. "Do Boyer think he can keep me from comin' through here with my cattle, he'll soon find out different. He knows we got the right o' way through here to the lake!"

Mrs. Boyer did not look up or reply. She kept on sprinkling flour.

🌷🌷🌷🌷🌷🌷🌷🌷🌷🌷🌷🌷🌷🌷🌷🌷🌷🌷🌷🌷🌷🌷🌷🌷

Slater stared at her and Birdie. Shoestring, beside him, stared too. Wide-eyed, they looked at the suspicious white powder on the strawberry plants.

Slater turned and spoke to Shoestring. He said only one word.

They wheeled their horses sharply and drove the cows off in another direction, skirting the fenced field, taking a longer, roundabout route to the lake. They let the new fence alone.

When Pa heard they'd come and gone without cutting the fence, he asked, "How did that happen?" He poked Ma in the ribs. "Did you use the little ole shotgun?"

"No," said Ma, "hit wasn't necessary. I just played a little trick on them. Now maybe we can live peaceable for a while." She let Birdie explain about the flour sacks.

"Flour!" exclaimed Pa. "Flour on the strawberry plants. What for? What did he think it was? What did he say?"

" 'Poison!' " said Ma.

CHAPTER IX

Strawberries

"THERE won't be no more cow squabbles for a while, anyway," said Mrs. Slater.

"And no more fence cutting," added Mrs. Boyer.

"You mighty right," said Mrs. Slater, with a sigh.

Mrs. Slater had come over to call as soon as the boys drove off with the cows.

The winter pasture was not good. The cattle could not get enough to eat. So Boyer and Slater forgot their differences and decided to have the boys drive their cows twenty-five miles to Lake Weller, where winter grass was better.

"I'm jest pinin' for egg custard," said Mrs. Slater. "Seems like I can't stand it, do I have to live another day without. I ain't seen milk for so long . . ."

"With all them cows? Three hundred?" asked Mrs. Boyer.

"Oh, them ain't milk cows, them's beef cattle—some calves and some yearlings," said Mrs. Slater.

"Your baby and little girls belong to have milk to drink," said Mrs. Boyer. "They look right puny."

"We had a milk cow once," sighed Mrs. Slater, "but she give so little, hit war a waste o' time to milk her."

[104]

❦❦❦❦❦❦❦❦❦❦❦❦❦❦❦❦❦❦❦❦❦❦❦❦❦❦❦❦

Mrs. Boyer turned to Birdie. "Go milk Susie Belle." Then to her visitor: "You shall have your egg custard. Got eggs?"

"Yes, plenty hens," said Mrs. Slater.

Birdie took the milk bucket and went out.

"You got a cow?" asked Mrs. Slater in astonishment.

"Shore have," replied Mrs. Boyer.

"But I thought Buzz and Shoestring and Gus and Sam drove all your cows to Lake Weller with our'n!"

"All but one," said Mrs. Boyer. "We keep one cow up all the time."

"Up to the house? In winter?" asked Mrs. Slater. "What do she eat?"

"Corn and fodder and whatever we feed her."

"You mean you *feed* her?"

"Shore do," said Mrs. Boyer, "so we'll get plenty milk. We use all we want and I make butter."

Mrs. Slater glanced out the window. "What's she tied to that orange tree for? Why don't you leave her run loose?"

"Manure's good for the tree," explained Mrs. Boyer. "First I tie her to one tree, then move her to the next. The children gather 'cow-chips,' dried cow droppings, out in the pasture, and we dump them round the orange trees, too, to manure 'em."

"Why, I never see a cow from fall till spring," said Mrs. Slater. "Sam always drives 'em a fur piece for winter grass. Good riddance too. I purely hate havin' the critters prancin' round loose. Can't have me no flower beds nor nothin'." She

[105]

peered out again. "Who's that up in the orange tree?"

"Pa and Dan are picking oranges," said Mrs. Boyer. "The seedlings are fine now. We're sellin' 'em by the barrel. I'll give you some for the children, since you ain't got no grove."

"Shucks—oranges! We never eat them!" sniffed Mrs. Slater. "They don't appeal to our notion."

Birdie brought the milk in and filled a bucket for Mrs. Slater.

"Lawzy!" cried Mrs. Slater. "Keepin' a cow up all the time!"

"We'll soon be pickin' our first strawberries," said Birdie, filled with pride.

"I'll send some over soon's they're ripe," added Mrs. Boyer.

"Nothin' don't grow like hit belongs to," mourned Mrs. Slater. "Even sweet 'taters don't make this year. Strawberries! Why, ain't them strawberry plants dead yet?"

Mrs. Slater took the milk home with her and feasted her family on egg custard. After that, through the winter months, the Slaters were seldom seen or heard from. With the cows removed from the scene, life for the Boyers became peaceful— but busier than ever.

The strawberry plants were not dead yet. With the advent of cooler weather, they began to grow sturdy and to send out blossoms. Early in January, the fruit began to form and it was not long until it showed color.

"Ain't them right purty, Ma?"

Birdie brought the first cupful in and Ma made shortcake.

"I think that's jest plumb good," said Pa.

It wasn't long until the rows were covered with bright red

[106]

berries and Pa said they were ready to be picked. "Where's my strawberry family?" he inquired.

"Here!" "Here!" They all answered from Dixie down to Bunny. All but Buzz, who at seventeen considered himself too grown-up for such childish work.

All the schools in the neighborhood had closed right after Christmas. So many families were growing berries, it had been decided to give the children their vacation in the three winter months—the strawberry season—so they could pick berries. Throughout the strawberry area, the schools were soon to become known as "Strawberry Schools."

At first, it was fun to pick berries. The children enjoyed being out in the sun all day and running barefoot and having a good time while they worked. They picked into quart baskets which they called "cups." They knelt on their knees or sat in the sand or stood up and bent over. The sand which looked so white was really black underneath. It clung to the berries, it soiled bare legs and feet, hands and faces, dresses and overalls.

"You-all belong to have baths in the tin tub," said Ma.

"Or a swim in the lake," said Dan.

"Bunny!" called Dixie. "Get out o' that ant bed! Look at him, Ma, he's settin' down there rubbin' his feet. He's plumb covered with ants."

Dan pulled Bunny away, and the small boy began to jump over the rows. Then he settled down to build roads in his never-ending sand pile.

Each child had a row to pick. When Birdie finished hers, she

[107]

heard Dovey calling: "Whoever wants to can help me out when they get done. Birdie, come help me out!"

Birdie loaded the long wooden carrier with twelve piled-up cups and took them to the shed under the clump of banana trees. There, Ma did the sorting. First she washed the berries in a tub of water. Then she spread them out on a table which had a covering of burlap for a top, to drain them. She picked out the culls and packed the perfect berries in clean baskets, ready for selling.

Birdie returned to the field to hear Dovey's plaintive cry: "Help me out! Help me out!" The penalty of being the fastest picker was helping the slower pickers pick their rows. She helped Dovey.

"Going to sleep, Dan?" called Dixie. "This here ain't no bed."

Dan was stretched out full-length in the sand. He made a mark with his toe, reached as far as he could and made another mark with his fingers. "There!" he cried, "I picked a quart in my own length, less than six feet. Good pickin' that!"

By mid-morning, the picking wasn't much fun. The rows seemed endlessly long. Legs and arms and backs began to ache. The sun shone uncomfortably hot. All the children were tired and ready to stop.

There were only two more rows to pick when Shoestring Slater appeared. Over his shoulder he carried a long stick, which had a bag tied on the end. He was followed by a pack of barking and yelping dogs. The children forgot how tired they were.

"What you totin', Shoestring?" called Dan.

"Guess!" answered the boy.

❦❦❦❦❦❦❦❦❦❦❦❦❦❦❦❦❦❦❦❦❦❦❦❦❦❦❦❦❦

"Gamecock!" guessed Dan.

"Pussy-cat!" guessed Dovey.

"Baby coon!" guessed Dixie.

Birdie remembered the snake on her old Sunday hat. "Bet you got a little ole snake in there!" she said.

"You mighty right!" laughed Shoestring.

"A blacksnake?"

"No, a live rattler!" said the boy.

"No!" cried the children all together. "You wouldn't dare!"

"Tell us how you caught him," begged Dan.

"I went ramblin' in the scrub," said Shoestring in his usual bragging tone, "and I come to a little branch, where there was a lot of bushes growin', and my hound dog bayed a rattlesnake. I smelled him first, and in a minute I seed him. I cut me this long bamboo pole and I tied a good strong string 'bout three feet long on the end, with a loop dangling. Ole snake was afeard o' me now and started to run under a thicket. I jest swung my pole, looped the loop right over his head—not tight enough to choke him—pulled it up and dropped him in my sack. And thar he is!"

"O-o-o-oh!" cried Dovey. "Ain't you afeard he'll bite you?"

"What you fixin' to do with him?" asked Birdie, shivering.

"Put him in a cage. Make him a pet. Gentle him. Feed him."

"What you feed him?"

"Live rabbits!"

"Oh, no!" cried Birdie. "You wouldn't!"

"That's what they eat when they run loose," said Shoestring.

❦❦❦❦❦❦❦❦❦❦❦❦❦❦❦❦❦❦❦❦❦❦❦❦❦❦

"They don't eat only so often, about once every three or four months, so they don't take much feedin'. Coons now got to be fed every day. They're a nuisance."

"What become of the one you had?" asked Birdie.

"Hit stoled a bunch of Ma's eggs and cracked 'em," said Shoestring with a grin, "and made her rarin'. She 'lowed she wouldn't have it round the house no more, so I takened it off in the woods and let it go."

"Your Ma won't let you keep no little ole rattler round the house neither," said Dixie.

"Naw!" said Shoestring. "I'll put the cage down back where the huckleberries grow. She won't never know it's there." Then he went on boasting: "I can gentle a raccoon or a possum or even a razorback. Bet I can gentle this little ole snake till he gets to know me. Then he won't never strike!"

"Take him off in the scrub and turn him loose," said Dixie, disgusted. "Hit ain't no fun messin' up with rattlers, once you get bit!"

"You swell up and turn green and die!" warned Dan. "Better take a shotgun to him!"

"Do he git to know me, he won't never bite me," said Shoestring.

"Go turn him loose," repeated Dixie.

"And come and help us pick strawberries," added Birdie. "We need all the help we can get."

"Naw!" Shoestring looked at the strawberry plants and spat with disgust. "I ain't messin' with no strawberries!" He strolled away, whistling.

[112]

❧❧❧❧❧❧❧❧❧❧❧❧❧❧❧❧❧❧❧❧❧❧❧❧❧❧❧❧❧❧

There was good picking all week and Pa took the berries to town and sold them. He was proud of his first crop. Then, one day, the thermometer began to drop. By noon it was 35° and still going down.

"We can't let the plants freeze," said Pa. "We'll cover 'em up with pine straw."

Birdie was sick at heart. They had worked so hard over the berries. It seemed cruel to lose them just as they were ripening.

With Pa and Buzz and Dan, she went into the piney woods and helped gather up pine straw—dried needles from the long-leaf pine. They filled baskets with it and dumped them into the wagon. They hauled pine straw by the wagon load all evening.

While waiting in the woods for the wagon to return, Birdie noticed a pen built on high legs standing near a clump of huckleberry bushes. It was behind, but within walking distance of the Slater house. She wondered why they kept their chickens so far away. She went over to look. Her hands were cold. She had come out without putting on a coat. She began to shiver.

She walked round the bushes and looked in the pen. "Oh!" she cried.

Inside the pen, she saw a coiled-up rattlesnake. The diamond markings on its back were very plain. "Shoestring's rattler!" she exclaimed.

But it was not the snake which caused her astonishment. In the far corner of the pen she saw a little live brown rabbit. It was huddled in a ball, afraid for its life. Its nose quivered anxiously.

🌷🌷🌷🌷🌷🌷🌷🌷🌷🌷🌷🌷🌷🌷🌷🌷🌷🌷🌷🌷🌷🌷🌷🌷🌷🌷🌷🌷

"A live rabbit!" she cried aloud, with bitter scorn in her voice. "That's what he feeds it—live rabbits!"

She remembered the snake on her hat. She remembered the deadly hatred with which she had hated Shoestring Slater then. Now, as she looked at the poor scared rabbit, she hated him even more. She hated him enough to kill him, to fight him, to . . . Was her hatred strong enough to get the rabbit out of the pen?

She knew she must act at once, before her hatred cooled, before she had time to lose courage.

The snake was coiled up, dormant because of the cold weather, in one corner of the pen. Could it be trusted to stay that way? The rabbit was in the other corner, as far away as possible. The door, fastened with a wooden turn-button, was between.

She knew what the bite of a rattlesnake meant. She knew how

quickly they struck, and how great the danger, when no help was near. But she never thought of waiting till her father and Buzz returned. She never thought of herself at all.

She opened the door quickly. She thrust her head and arm inside. Keeping her eye on the snake, she grasped the rabbit firmly by its forelegs and pulled it out. The snake did not move. She closed the door and fastened the button. She took a deep breath, then she smiled and patted the rabbit on its head.

"Pore thing!" she said. "You purely been in hell. I'm givin' you your freedom!"

She dropped the rabbit to the ground. She saw that it was unharmed. She watched it go bounding off through the bushes. She wondered how many weeks it had been caged with the snake. The snake was not hungry. They ate only once in three or four months, Shoestring had said.

She shivered, then she cried. She put her hands to her face, and felt they were no longer cold. She was hot all over.

She felt better. She didn't hate Shoestring Slater any more.

After a little, she went back. Pa had returned with the wagon and she gathered more pine straw. She did not mention what she had done. When dark came down, Pa sent her and Dan back to the house to go to bed. He and Buzz worked far into the night covering the plants. The thermometer went down to 27°.

Several days later they raked the pine straw off, leaving it between the rows, for later use, if necessary. They waited for more blossoms to bear fruit. After the cold spell, the sun came out bright and warm to put color and ripeness and flavor into the berries. Pa's strawberry family began to pick regularly twice a week.

One day Shoestring came. He hung over the fence and stared at the beautiful red berries.

"Come help us pick!" cried Dan.

"Naw!" said the boy.

"Big ole lazy you!" teased Birdie.

"How's your pet snake?" asked Dan. "Learn him any tricks?"

"Naw!" said Shoestring. He spat in the sand.

"Got snake-bit yet?" asked Dixie.

"Naw!"

"Your snake hungry?" asked Birdie.

"Naw!"

"Fed him ary live rabbits lately?"

"Naw! He et one up, slick as a whistle, didn't leave a hair. He warn't hungry at first. Rabbit was in his pen a whole week before he swallered it."

"I purely don't believe it!" said Birdie.

"Fixin' to git him another?" asked Dan.

"Naw!"

"Why not?"

"Snake's dead!" said Shoestring. "Froze hisself to death."

"Is he done dead?" asked Dan. "Likely he's jest sleepin'."

"Naw! Dead. Froze stiff," said Shoestring.

Birdie was glad the snake was dead. It had had no place to hibernate, in an open pen like that. She decided she might as well tell Shoestring what she had done.

"Your snake never et that rabbit!" she announced.

"What?" They all looked at her. Shoestring opened his mouth and stared. "How you know?"

"I done opened the door and let it out!"

"You done that?" gasped Shoestring. "You jest better let my snake alone!" He paused, then he added, "Ain't you got no sense at all? You could a been bit to death. Wal—snake's dead anyhow!" He walked off, shoulders hunched and his hands deep in his overall pockets.

Strawberry picking continued good, and they all thought that the worst trials were over. It was a complete surprise, and it seemed the last straw, therefore, to come out one morning, as Birdie did, and find the field covered with robins—fat, saucy, red-breasted robins. A huge flock, migrating to their northern homes for the summer months, had stopped for a dainty meal on the way.

"Shoo! Shoo!" cried Birdie, waving her apron in the air. "Shoo away! Go visit the Yankees!"

The children threw stones and brandished sticks. Dan tried to trap the robins. Buzz put up poles and tied streamers of cloth on them to wave in the wind. Ma shook her broom. Pa shot his shotgun into the air. The robins flew up, it is true, but they flew right down again. They did not leave the field until they had stripped it of every ripe berry.

The next day the birds did not come. They did not come because there were no ripe berries for them to eat. And there were none for the children to pick.

CHAPTER X

Alligator

WE must hurry," said Pa, one Thursday. "We picked so many strawberries this mornin', we're mighty late. Reckon we'll miss that train iffen we don't mind out."

Birdie put on her new Sunday hat and ran to the wagon.

"No more shipping in wooden crates," said Pa. "Our pony refrigerators will be ready this week. Now we can raise berries in quantity and get them to our customers up north the third day after they are picked—and on ice!"

The strawberry growers had had meetings to discuss better schemes for shipping their berries. They had ordered iceboxes made for each shipper. Thursday of each week was the biggest shipping day.

The horse, Osceola, started at a walk, unwilling to trot. No amount of whipping would speed him up.

"Gittin' lazy like ole Semina!" said Pa. "Needs a spring tonic of some kind. But Lordy, we mustn't miss that train!" He turned to Birdie on the seat beside him. "Do we miss it, gal, you'll have to sell the berries out on the street corner."

Birdie laughed. "Sixty-four quarts! Who would buy them all?"

"Or likely peddle 'em from house to house," added Pa, with a chuckle.

"Like old Janey Pokes!" laughed Birdie. "I hope we won't come to that, now we got us a Pony Refrigerator 'at cost twelve dollars!"

Recent rains had drained through the sand, leveled the ruts and packed the road. The wagon wheels rolled smoothly, and the horse's hoofs made gentle thuds. Farther on, through the

❦❦❦❦❦❦❦❦❦❦❦❦❦❦❦❦❦❦❦❦❦❦❦❦❦❦❦

piney woods, Osceola trotted over beds of soft pine needles.

Beyond the woods, the road passed through a forest of cypress trees which had their roots in a boggy swamp of black, stagnant water. A corduroy road of rough logs had been built to cross it. The rains had raised the water level almost up to that of the road.

Pa touched Osceola's back lightly with the whip and urged him on. The horse stopped, for the way was completely blocked. A monster alligator was waddling across the road just ahead.

"Looky yonder!" said Pa. "That feller's just woke up from his winter's nap. He knows 'at spring is here. Lordy, I wisht I had my shotgun. Did I bring it with me, we'd have alligator steak for supper!"

"But you ain't got it," said Birdie. "What you fixin' to do, Pa?"

"Can't pass him, that's a fact," said Pa, frowning.

"Not without us rollin' off into the black swamp and takin' a bath!" added Birdie. "Ugh!"

"Jest gotta back up and wait till he makes up his mind where he's goin'!" Pa gave a half-hearted laugh. "Every minute's worth money, too, with that train comin' in right on the dot. Never late neither."

Pa backed Osceola to a safe distance. The alligator rose up on his feet, kept his head turned toward the intruders, and his huge mouth partly open. He lifted his tail to one-half his length, ready to flay an unwelcome visitor at a moment's warning.

"Good thing the dogs didn't come along," said Pa. "That ole 'gator shore would like a big mouthful of dog!"

"Or hog!" added Birdie.

Osceola pranced nervously while they waited. Finally the alligator waddled off into the black depths of the cypress swamp.

Pa did not need to whip up the horse. As if anxious to get away from the beast in the swamp, Osceola made a swift dash for town. They arrived just as the train whistle sounded in the distance.

Birdie had never been in the depot before. It was a busy place when strawberries were coming in. People were waiting for the mail or getting paid for their produce or just visiting, while strawberry growers unloaded on the platform and packed their fruit. There was a great deal of bustle and confusion, and Station Master Jenkins had his hands full. With a pencil behind his ear, he ran back and forth like a distracted hen.

[122]

"Where's that new icebox of mine?" called Mr. Boyer.

Jenkins pointed to a long row of them. Old Simon, a crippled colored man, had brought ice for everybody in his two-mule wagon, and was carrying it in.

Birdie helped Pa load the Pony Refrigerator. It had a double wall of cypress lumber and was painted white. On the side, large letters were printed: NO. 42 SHIPPED BY BIHU BOYER TO EVERGREEN STRAWBERRY CO., PHILADELPHIA. Birdie handed up the quarts and Pa packed them in. It held sixty-four. On top was an ice pan six inches deep, with a center pan for ventilation, through which the melting ice dripped.

"Pa!" said Birdie. "Do hit go away on the train?"

"Shore, sugar! All the way to Philadelphia! Next year we'll send them Yankees some big fat berries in time for Christmas and make 'em pay us a dollar a quart!"

Birdie was still puzzled. "What will you ship your berries in next week after the refrigerator's gone away on the train?"

"Honey," said Pa, "this little ole Pony's comin' back by the very first train south. The railroad brings it back free o' charge. Then I load her up and send her off again. Them Yankees git their berries fresh like the dew's still on 'em!"

"Now I tell you what!" A loud-voiced man approached. "You strawberry growers are makin' a big mistake by puttin' your berries up in quarts. You could charge and git twice as much for 'em if you'd pack 'em in pints."

Pa looked up inquiringly.

"You a stranger here?" he asked.

"Yes," said the man, "from Louisiana. We pack in pints there."

Somebody spoke up. "Folk'd buy only one pint, not two. As it is, they can't never buy less than a quart."

Mr. Boyer added: "Large berries like mine don't pack so good in pints. Two big berries are not enough to go across the top of a pint cup, and three big ones are too much. Quarts are better. See that quart there? It's got just thirteen berries over the top."

"Some day you'll change to pints," said the stranger.

"And make a big mistake," added Boyer.

The station master began shouting. The refrigerators were quickly rolled up into the freight car, the door was closed and locked, and the car was hooked on behind the train. Soon the strawberries were on their way to the far north, and Pa and Birdie were on their way home again.

All the way home, Pa felt cheerful because he had sold so many berries. He began to sing and Birdie joined in:

> "Jaybird sittin' on a swingin' limb,
> swingin' limb,
> swingin' limb!
> Jaybird sittin' on a swingin' limb,
> High oh, high oh, high oh!
>
> I picked up a rock and hit him on the chin,
> hit him on the chin,
> hit him on the chin!
> I picked up a rock and hit him on the chin,
> High oh, high oh, high oh!

> Looky here, my little man, don't you do that agin,
>   don't you do that agin,
>   don't you do that agin!
> Looky here, my little man, don't you do that agin,
>   High oh, high oh, high oh!''

They sang at the top of their voices and were very happy together. Pa started off on another song, but stopped in the middle of a line. "Look yonder!" he said, pointing.

They had returned to the cypress swamp, where they saw buzzards circling above the feathery green foliage of the trees. The great black birds swooped down to the ground and then up again.

"That big ole 'gator been killed?" asked Birdie.

"He might could," said Pa, "walkin' out on the road that way, did some man come along with a shotgun on his shoulder."

But the alligator was not in sight. Instead, in the marshy grass at the edge of the swamp, a cow was bogged up to her neck. She mooed in distress, as the greedy buzzards all but lighted on her head.

"Pore thing!" cried Birdie. "Oh, Pa, the buzzards are after her and she's still alive. Iffen she moves, she's shore to sink."

"That's what happens when you have Open Range," said Pa angrily. "Cows go everywhere, and the owner never knows how many he loses. Better keep 'em fenced up and give 'em a little care." He paused. "Did I fetch my shotgun, I'd shoot her quick to end her misery. Or did I have a rope . . ." He jumped from the wagon.

"What you fixin' to do, Pa?" asked Birdie. "Kin I help?"

"No, sugar. Stay where you air."

He went to a tree and began pulling down a great length of heavy grapevine, which was growing up the trunk. He cut it loose, made a loop in one end and threw it over the cow's head. After several tries, he succeeded in lassoing the animal. Then he pulled slowly and steadily until she gradually regained her footing, and came up on the more solid bank of the road.

He knocked mud off her, looked at her ear-mark and then saw that her brand was the circle S.

"Hit's Slater's cow!" he said. "Likely he won't even thank me for savin' her life."

"The buzzards have all gone away," said Birdie.

"Gone back to town to sit on the tops of the chimneys," said Pa, "to swoop down and git the garbage folkses throw out. Them birds ain't exactly choice what food they eat. They got cheated out of a good dinner here."

Pa used the grapevine to tie the rescued cow to the rear of the wagon. Osceola started on.

They went first to the Slaters.

At first they thought there was nobody at home, then Mrs. Slater came out on the porch with her baby slung on her hip. "Howdy!" she said.

"Found one of your cows bogged up in the cypress swamp," explained Mr. Boyer. "I pulled her out and brung her home behind my wagon."

He untied the grapevine. The animal was covered with

[126]

black, mucky slime and was hardly able to stand on her feet. Under the muck, she looked thin and bony. Mrs. Slater stared at her.

"Don't look like none of our'n," she said.

"She's got your markin' brand, circle S," said Boyer. "She belongs to be scrubbed off and fed up and took care of for a week or two."

"Can't do that," said the woman.

"Your men folks can," said Boyer.

"All gone off," replied Mrs. Slater. "Ain't worth it, nohow."

"She needs water to drink," said Boyer.

"I wouldn't tote a bucket o' water for no cow on earth," said the woman. "I purely hate cattle."

"She's worth ten or twelve dollars, do you feed her up a bit," said Boyer.

"I'd not see ary penny of it, did they sell her."

"I'd as good to let her bog down and die, then, in the swamp," said Boyer crossly. "You got feed for her?"

"I never see ary cow worth feedin' or totin' water for," insisted Mrs. Slater.

Shoestring came round the house and stopped when he heard voices. He had a fish—a bream—in his hands.

"Hey, Birdie!" he called. "See what I got! Dropped right down from the sky!"

"Huh!" said Birdie. "Expect me to believe that? You been fishin'."

"I was down yonder by the lake," said the boy, "and I looked

up and heard a loud squallin' and I see a bream flyin' through the air. I held out my hat and caught it and here it is!"

"You caught it on a hook!" said Birdie.

"Naw-sir-ree!" Shoestring continued in a boastful tone. "Fish hawk dove down in the lake and caught him this fish. Ole eagle was settin' on a dead limb watchin'. When the fish hawk started off with it, the eagle flew up and hit him in the back and they had a fight and made a terrible noise. The eagle got the fish away from the fish hawk, but when he seen me and heard me holler at him, he got scared and dropped the fish —right in my hat! Neither of 'em will eat this fish for supper— I will."

"Looky here, son!" said Mr. Boyer, pointing. "That cow belongs to be scrubbed clean, fed and watered and looked after."

Shoestring stared at the animal. "She shore do!" he said.

"Never did a stroke of work in your life, did you, son?" asked Boyer.

"No sir—I mean, yes sir!" said the boy.

"Hit's your Pa's cow," said Boyer. "He and your brothers are gone off. Can't you . . ."

"I ain't messin' up with no cows!" said Shoestring, shrugging his shoulders.

"I thought you was a cowman and rode a cowhorse," said Birdie.

"Hit's fun to ride a horse . . ."

"So you ain't messin' up with no cows!" Like a gust of mighty wind, Mr. Boyer's anger rose. "Well, you air! But first

I'll whop you good to make shore!"

He grabbed the boy by the shirt collar, pulled a strong but limber branch off a tree and began to lay on strenuous blows. The fish flew up in the air and fell again on the sand. Shoestring yelled at the top of his voice.

Mrs. Slater screamed, "You're killin' him! You're killin' him! You leave my pore Jeff alone!" The baby on her hip cried lustily and Essie and Zephy came running out. "Don't you hurt our Jeffie! Don't you hurt our Jeffie!" they screamed.

But Mr. Boyer did not stop until he had done a thorough job.

"Now you do what I tell you to!"

He stood over the whimpering boy and told him how to take care of the cow. After he had seen the animal comfortably installed in the shelter behind the house, he was ready to leave.

Birdie had stood by and watched it all. She knew how much her father loved animals and insisted on proper care and feed for them—even if they were not his own. She herself could not bear to see an animal suffer without wanting to help it. She wanted the poor cow to be taken care of, after its narrow escape. But she also knew that the Slaters would never forgive Pa for whipping Shoestring. It would be harder than ever to be friends with them after this.

Essie and Zephy rushed out and beat at her with their fists. They told her to go away and not come back. She had always been kind to the two little girls, no matter what their parents did. She thought they were her friends. Now they began throwing sticks at her new Sunday hat.

Quickly she climbed up into the wagon seat beside Pa. Mrs. Slater was still scolding at the top of her voice.

"All you folks do is make trouble!" she wailed. "After what your wife done . . ."

Boyer let the reins drop. "What's *she* done?" he asked quietly.

"She bought herself a Bible from that feller who come around sellin' 'em," said Mrs. Slater.

"What's wrong with that?" asked Boyer.

"The Bible-sellin' feller done tole me she bought one, so I was obliged to buy one too."

"Why on earth?" asked the man, puzzled. "Nobody's forcin' you to buy a Bible iffen you don't want one. But it might do ye a heap o' good to read it now and then. Did you not want it, why buy it?"

"I heard tell hit's unlucky not to buy one," admitted Mrs. Slater.

"Wal—read it then," said Boyer. "Hit says somethin' about lovin' your neighbor." He picked up the reins and drove off.

CHAPTER XI

Spotted Calf

*T*HINGS were pretty quiet for the rest of the winter.

"I wisht them cows would never come back," said Mrs. Boyer, "so we might could go on livin' peaceable."

"So do I, Ma," said Birdie.

But they were not to have their wish. The return of the cattle from Lake Weller in the spring stirred up immediate trouble. Things began to happen fast. It began with the spotted heifer calf.

Buzz and the Slater boys, Gus, Joe and Shoestring, went on the cow hunt to bring the cattle back. They were gone ten days, rounding up the cows that had strayed. One of the Boyers' cows could not be found. After several days they located her several miles away from the others. She had a pretty spotted heifer calf.

When the boys got back, the Boyers all came out to see the calves.

"We got to brand 'em right away," Pa said, "before anybody gets their hands on 'em."

Pa felt good to see so many. He tossed Bunny up in the air.

"The spotted calf belongs to Bunny," he said. "Can't start

[133]

too young to make a cowman out of him. Time the boy's growed, he'll have a herd of his own."

"Pa's brand was the double B brand: BB for Bihu Boyer. He created a new one for Bunny; the diamond B: ⬦ . The first time he went to town, he had a branding iron made at the blacksmith shop, with the new mark on it. On the day of the branding, he made a fire of lightwood knots in the barnyard, and put the branding irons in to heat.

Buzz and Dan had fenced the calves away from their mothers, in one of the cowpens. Now they brought them out one at a time. Joe Slater came over to help. Birdie and Dovey hung over the fence to watch.

The men took one calf at a time. Joe threw it to the ground, Buzz put his knee on the calf's neck, then Joe and Dan held its feet. Pa took the red hot iron from the fire and pressed it firmly on the calf's hip, just long enough to make the mark. The burned hair and flesh smoked and smelled, while the calf blatted piteously.

It made Birdie feel sick. She turned to go into the house. Then she heard Pa calling for the spotted calf, the one that was to be Bunny's. She waited to see what the new marking brand would look like.

Buzz and Dan had not seen the calf since they penned the others up. Joe Slater insisted he didn't even know they had a spotted heifer. Pa looked at Joe suspiciously and wondered why he was so sure about it.

Birdie and Dovey went to look for the calf. It was not in the pen or the crib. They looked in the pasture and the fields, but could not find it anywhere. The mother cow set up a noisy bawling.

Buzz decided to go on a cow hunt. He got the horse out, and rode through the woods and scrub, hunting for the calf. He took the hunting dogs along to trail it, in case it had been carried off by some wild beast. It was late that night when he returned.

"I ain't seen hide nor hair of that calf," he said grimly. "It ain't been killed. Somebody's takened it. That's shore."

Pa frowned. The loss of a heifer calf was serious.

"Remember what Joe said?" asked Buzz. "Said he didn't even know we had a spotted heifer!"

❦❦❦❦❦❦❦❦❦❦❦❦❦❦❦❦❦❦❦❦❦❦❦❦❦❦❦

"Now jest why did Joe say that?" asked Pa.

It was Birdie who answered his question.

She came tearing home the next day, running as fast as the wind.

"What's after you, gal young un?" demanded Pa, smiling. "Bear? Wildcat? Alligator? Must be somethin' fierce to make you run so fast!"

"Pa! Pa!" Birdie stopped to catch breath. "Pa, I saw the spotted heifer calf! Hit's got Slaters' markin' brand on it, the circle S! Like this!" She leaned over and drew the mark in the sand with her finger: ⑤ . "And Essie done told me their mother cow's got two calves. I seen 'em both, and they ain't twins. T'other calf's a head taller'n the spotted one."

Pa's lips closed in a tight line.

"Sugar, how did you happen to see all this?" he asked. All the family crowded round to hear Birdie's answer.

"Ma sent me over to the Slaters'," said she, "to ask could I bring back the clothespins Mrs. Slater borrowed. There warn't nobody in their house. They was all out back, where the men was brandin' calves. I didn't want to see no more brandin', so when I see the little girls playin' near the shelter back o' the house, I went over and asked 'em could I take back Ma's clothespins. They was still mad, count of you whopped Shoestring, but they talked to me anyhow.

"Right there in the shelter, I see our spotted heifer calf and t'other one. Essie done tole me the mother cow had got two calves. And Zephy explained. She said her Pa penned the first calf up and turned its mother loose for a few days. When the mother cow come back home, she had another calf with her—the spotted one. Now she's got two! And they both got Slaters' markin' brand on 'em.''

"What did you do then?" asked Pa.

"I found the clothespins on the back porch and I was jest startin' for home when Shoestring seen me. He ain't spoke to me since you whopped him, Pa. 'What you doin',' he says. 'Stealin' clothespins?' 'They're my Ma's,' says I, 'and my Ma said your Ma had kept 'em long enough and for me to go fetch 'em back.' He said, 'You jest better leave our clothespins alone! You're always meddlin' in other folkses' business.' I says, 'Well, I don't steal things like you Slaters do!'

" 'What do we steal?' asks Shoestring and I says, 'Bunny's spotted heifer and you know it. You penned her own calf away from that mother cow so she'd go out and find another and she brung in our spotted heifer and your Pa branded it with your markin' brand, but hit's our'n, hit's Bunny's!' I says. 'You stoled it!' "

Birdie stopped, flushed with anger.

"Sugar," said Pa quietly, "hit war a waste o' breath to say all that to the boy. What'd he answer?"

"He said the calf belonged to their cow and not to Bunny," said Birdie. "He called me a liar. He chunked pine knots at me all the way home."

"Honey, he might a hit ye and hurted ye," said Pa. "Hit don't pay to sass them Slater folks."

[137]

"I don't care noways at all," said Birdie. "That calf's Bunny's."

Pa looked very serious. He did not speak.

"Can he keep Bunny's calf," asked Birdie, "now he's put the Slater brand on it?"

"I reckon so," said Pa quietly. "Can't nobody go changin' brands without landin in jail."

As if things were not bad enough already, the Slater hogs began to come round again. They were tame enough now. They came to the back door sniffing for slops and Birdie had to drag them away and put them outside the fence. Perhaps Shoe-string had stopped feeding them and they had resumed their wild ways. They could get under any fence in the world and they began to root up crops in the Boyers' fields.

A night came when the air was filled with squealing and

[138]

whacking. Birdie woke to hear it and shivered with dread. The hogs were inside the fence, and this time Pa was good and angry because of the loss of the heifer calf. This time, Birdie knew, Pa would do more than mark a hog's ears and send it home for a warning.

Birdie ducked under the covers to shut the sounds out. Even then she could hear, so she put her fingers in her ears. Silence came at last, and she fell asleep. In the morning, she woke early, thinking she heard footsteps on the porch. She came out in the early dawn.

There were Essie and Zephy Slater scuttling down the steps like scared rabbits and running towards the palmetto bushes.

"What you-all doin' here?" cried Birdie. She ran after them, and grabbed them by the arms. "What you been doin' on our porch so early in the mornin'? Why, it ain't even light yet!"

"We can't tell . . ." wailed Essie.

"Hit's a secret," added Zephy.

Essie's eyes were red and Zephy began to cry.

"What you-all cryin' for?" repeated Birdie. "You-all come tell me." She dragged them back to the porch steps.

"Pa's fightin' mad at you-uns," said Essie.

"What for?" Birdie's heart began to pound.

"They're dead," said Zephy.

"What are?" asked Birdie patiently.

"The two calves?

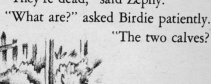

The spotted heifer and t'other one?"

"No," said Essie. "Three hogs."

"They got our mark in the ears, so they're our'n," added Zephy.

"Pa found 'em dead on our front porch," said Essie, "when he got up this mornin'."

Birdie gasped. Now she knew how angry her father must have been last night. Pa had killed three of Slater's hogs, the way he said he would. All because of the spotted calf.

"There!" Essie pointed to a folded paper which she had tucked under the front door. "That's what we come for—Pa made us bring it."

Birdie picked it up with trembling fingers.

Like pale shadows, the little girls scuttled off and disappeared in the clump of palmetto bushes, which was the short cut between the two homes. Birdie looked down at the paper in her hand. She opened it. It was written in Gus's uncertain handwriting, but the meaning of the words was plain. The note said: *Will git you yet iffen we got to burn you out!* There was no name signed to it.

Another cowardly note. Sam Slater was afraid to face her father. Should she tear it to bits like the former one? No, this time she did not dare. Sam Slater was really angry this time. He would not let things slide as he did before. Her father must know.

She folded the note carefully. She found her father at the pump on the back porch. She waited till he dried his face and hands on the roller towel. She studied his face while he read the note, and she saw it turn grave.

"Pa . . ." she began uncertainly, "do you jest love a ruckus, like Ma said?"

"Now, sugar," he said, tipping up her chin, "don't you get worried, a weensy gal like you, no bigger'n a hummin' bird. Don't you know your Pa can take care of this?"

"He'll git his shotgun, Pa . . ."

Pa laughed. "Want to go to town with me today?" he asked. "We mustn't forget our strawberries. And there's two to three barrels of oranges Buzz picked. Got to ship 'em to them Yankees up north."

"But you jest purely can't go away and leave things today, Pa," said Birdie. "Something might could happen."

"No harm in broad daylight," said Pa. "Cowards like him only work at night."

Birdie tried to feel comforted, but she could not get over her uneasiness. She was glad to have the chance to go to town.

There were not many strawberries to pick that morning, as the end of the season was at hand. The oranges had been packed the day before. Pa was in a hurry to start, so Birdie went just as she was—with her feet bare, and her sunbonnet.

Pa said it was not worth taking half a crate of strawberries to the depot for shipping. So Birdie stood at the corner by the square and sold them to passers-by. When she saw Miss Liddy coming, she wished she had put on her shoes and stockings and worn her Sunday hat.

[141]

"Oh, here's the Strawberry Girl!" said Miss Liddy. She bought two quarts. "Where's your wagon and your bell? I thought you were going to ride around like old Janey Pokes!"

"Pa said standin' at the corner was better, ma'am." Birdie smiled. It was always nice to see Miss Liddy.

"Any more fence cutting out your way?" inquired Miss Liddy.

"No ma'am," said Birdie.

"Fighting never settles anything," said Miss Liddy.

"That's what Ma always says."

"I'm glad your father and Mr. Slater have come to their senses and are good friends again," said Miss Liddy.

"Yes ma'am," said Birdie.

"I felt sure a fine man like your father would be a good influence on poor Mr. Slater," said Miss Liddy.

"Yes ma'am," said Birdie.

Birdie wondered what Miss Liddy would think if she knew that Pa had killed three of Slater's hogs the night before. She wondered if Slater were in town, and if he and Pa would meet somewhere and fight again. She wondered if Slater would beat the starch out of Pa this time. No—Pa was bigger and stronger. But Miss Liddy was right—fighting never settled anything.

A woman stopped and Birdie had to think about strawberries again. Other people passed and most of them bought. They all called her Strawberry Girl and said the berries were extra good for so late in the season.

Pa came just as she was selling the last quart. She did not have to wait for him. He did not have a black eye, so she guessed he had not been fighting. Slater must have stayed at home today. Had he made trouble there?

When they got home, the first thing they saw was that Ma had not plowed up the strawberry rows after all. She had said she would do the plowing and keep an eye on the place.

They went in the kitchen and supper was not ready. Dixie was just peeling the potatoes. There sat Ma on a chair doing nothing. She had her apron lifted up to her face and she was crying in it. Dovey and Bunny were crying too.

Birdie had never seen Ma cry before, so she knew something dreadful had happened.

"What's the matter, wife?" Pa put his hand on her shoulder and spoke kindly.

"Let's go back home to Caroliny," sobbed Ma. "We can't never live peaceable here in Floridy, where there's sich goin's-on . . ."

"What happened?" asked Pa. "Has . . ."

"Semina's dead!" announced Ma.

"Now we ain't got nary mule," said Dovey.

"I found her lyin' dead out in the pasture," said Dan. "I poked her with a stick but she wouldn't move."

"Poor Semina!" said Pa. "Her balkin' days are over. Wal— she was bound to die sometime. Can't expect a mule to live forever."

Ma dropped her apron and stood up. "Slater done it," she said.

"You shore?" asked Pa, frowning.

"Dan and I went out to the pasture to git her for the plowin'," explained Ma, "and I found little piles of feed out there, covered with Paris green. Semina et some of it and hit killed her. She was poisoned. I saw Slater hangin' over the fence. He yelled out: 'Poison.' I thought he was talkin' about the flour I put on the strawberry plants that time to scare off his cows. I didn't know what he meant till I found Paris green all over pore Semina's mouth."

"In broad daylight!" exclaimed Pa. "He's a worse skunk than I thought."

"Oh, why did you kill them hogs?" cried Ma. "As long as you go on payin' him back, we'll never be able to live peaceable. It will jest be one ruckus after another. He can always think of somethin' worse to do."

"I purely can't let him walk right over me," said Pa. He

put his arm around Ma's shoulders. "One day, all this trouble will come to an end," he assured her.

"Jest when we thought we was gittin' ahead . . ." said Ma.

"We are gittin' ahead," said Pa. "We done well with our oranges, and if we fertilize 'em good, we'll do better next year. We made more on our strawberries than ary person I met in town. Tomorrow we'll plow up the field and get it ready to reset it with new plants. Next year we'll make twice as much."

"How can we plow without Semina?" wailed Birdie.

"We still got a horse," said Pa. "Good thing I took Osceola to town today. It might could a been the horse got poisoned. I'll git us a new mule next time I go to town—trade in a cow or two. There's always a way to git ahead when you've got a mind to!"

They all went out to the pasture and looked at the white mule lying stretched out on the ground. Buzz and Pa dug a big hole to bury her.

"Pore ole Semina!" said Birdie.

CHAPTER XII

Grass Fire

HER name's Speckle," said Birdie. "She comes when I call."
A speckled hen walked across the porch, followed by ten
baby chicks. "Here, you come here, Speckle!"

The hen was quite tame. It jumped on Birdie's knee, then
climbed to her shoulder. She held some grains of corn in her
hand and the hen gobbled them up. Then it began to peck her
ear. "Hey! Don't do that! Don't hurt me!"

Essie and Zephy were friendly again. They had come to
play with Dovey and Bunny.

"Once Speckle got a cold," said Birdie. "So I rubbed her
throat every day. I poured medicine down till she got well."

"Speckle sleeps in Birdie's room," said Dovey.

"I leave the door open," said Birdie, "so she can come in and
go out when she wants to. I made her a nest on a pile of rags
under my bed, and she laid an egg there every day."

"And hatched 'em into biddies?" asked Zephy.

❧❧❧❧❧❧❧❧❧❧❧❧❧❧❧❧❧❧❧❧❧❧❧❧❧❧❧

"Yes, she sot on 'em for three weeks," said Birdie. "Now I got ten biddies. I'll gentle 'em too, just like Speckle."

Mrs. Boyer was starting a fire under the washpot in the yard.

"Birdie," she called, "go help Buzz with that painting or he'll never git done. You can work from the stepladder and do the low part."

"Let's git our play-dollies," said Dovey. The children walked round the house, and the hen and chicks wandered off.

The time had come to paint the house, though Pa had bought the paint months before. Birdie climbed up on the ladder and set to work. She slapped her paintbrush up and down noisily. It was good to see one plank after another change from its weathered gray to a pearly white. No one would recognize the old Roddenberry house when they got through. Soon it would be called the Boyers' white house. How pretty the box-flowers would look on the porch all white and shiny!

"Gettin' biggety, ain't ye?"

It was Shoestring Slater who spoke. He stood at the foot of the ladder and gave it a shake.

"Go 'long!" cried Birdie. "Git away 'fore I drop a bucket of paint down your neck!"

"Think you're better'n other people, don't ye!" the boy went on.

But just then Buzz came round the house with the high ladder, so Shoestring disappeared.

In the middle of the morning, Buzz was called away to help his father. Birdie kept on painting. Her arms ached from lifting the heavy brush. Her legs ached from climbing up and

[147]

down the ladder. Her face, arms, legs and dress were spattered with white paint. The side of the house seemed endlessly large and the sun was hot.

No one was around. The children had gone into the palmetto tunnel, where it was cool, to play.

Suddenly Birdie smelled smoke. At first she thought it was the fire under the washpot. Then, from the top of the ladder, she noticed the pine smell and saw a cloud of smoke rising in the flatwoods pasture. Was it a forest or a grass fire? Perhaps turpentine and lumbermen had set it to drive out snakes, so the Negro workers would not be afraid to slash the pine trees and set buckets for turpentine. Perhaps cattlemen had set it, to burn off the dead grass so the cattle could get at the new growth.

Birdie shaded her eyes with her hand and studied about it. She saw that the fire was between the Slaters' and the Boyers' places. The turpentine men worked farther to the north. Cattlemen—well, if it were set by cattlemen, it could be nobody but Sam Slater. He was the only real cattleman around. All the other neighbors were farmers. They had farms and a bunch of cattle too, but not a big herd like Slater's.

Birdie's face grew serious as she watched. Why should she think somebody had set the fire on purpose? Why was she always so suspicious? Fires often started by accident. Maybe somebody built a bonfire and forgot to put it out.

Anyhow it did not concern her. She turned her back and began to paint the house. She worked fast, thinking how

❧❧❧❧❧❧❧❧❧❧❧❧❧❧❧❧❧❧❧❧❧❧❧❧❧❧❧❧❧

pretty the house would look when it was done.

Then she smelled the smoke again. She dropped the paint-brush in the bucket, as she saw a billowy cloud of smoke sweeping through the piney woods and all through the pasture. It was a grass fire, but the pine trees were burning too. It was moving forward rapidly. She could hear it popping and crackling.

"Ma! Pa! Dixie, Buzz, Dan!" she called. She jumped off the ladder and raced round the house, shouting: "The piney woods is afire!"

Pa and Buzz were nowhere to be seen. Ma and Dixie were washing clothes in the backyard. Dixie stood over the wash-pot, stirring the boiling clothes with a long stick. Ma leaned over the block—a big stump about three feet high—where she had laid some of the dirtiest of the men's clothes, wetted and soaped. She pounded them vigorously with the battling stick. Several tubs and a trough, made from a hollowed-out log, stood near by, filled with water.

Ma and Dixie did not need to be called twice. When they saw the cloud of smoke approaching the house, they seized buckets, dipped them in the tubs of water, and sped out to the pasture, running.

"Get sacks from the crib!" called Ma. "And wet 'em! You, Dan, pump more water and keep the tubs filled!"

"Where's Pa? Where's Buzz? Where they gone to?" wailed Birdie.

Nobody knew. They all ran out to fight the fire. It was close now and coming steadily closer. The grass was burning, setting fire to clumps of palmettos. A loud swoosh and noisy crackle

❦❦❦❦❦❦❦❦❦❦❦❦❦❦❦❦❦❦❦❦❦❦❦❦❦❦❦❦❦

burst out as each new clump of palmetto flared up in flames.

They poured water on the fire, but it did little or no good. The dampened sacks were better. They beat the burning grass with them and thought they were making headway, until they looked and saw that the line of fire was only moving off in other directions. It was about to encircle the house.

"The house!" cried Birdie. "The house will burn!"

All their work to make a new home would be lost if it went up in smoke. Birdie felt sick inside. Would it never get its coat of shiny white paint?

"Birdie!" gasped Ma. "We got to git help. Do it come closer to the house, we can't save it. Get on the horse and ride to the Slaters' and ask 'em all to come quick!"

Birdie flew. She threw herself on Osceola's back and began pounding him on the rump. The horse, sensing danger, picked up his heels. But he would not ride through the smoke. He kept turning and backing. Birdie chose a roundabout course, skirting the flames, and rode as fast as she could to the Slater house.

She saw Sam and Gus and Joe sitting on the front porch. She began to yell, "Fire! Fire! Come and put out the fire!"

They could not help but hear her.

They could not help but see and smell the smoke. They must have done so before she came riding up.

But they did not move. They sat on their slat-backed chairs, tipped against the wall of the house, as if they had not a care in the world.

Birdie pulled up her horse at their front steps. "The piney

[151]

woods is all afire!" she cried. "We need your help mighty bad! Do hit get any worse, our house will burn up!" In imagination she could see the Roddenberry house a heap of black and charred ashes.

"A grass fire's a mighty good thing in the spring," said Sam Slater slowly. "Hit's good for greenin' up the woods for the cattle!"

"But our house is burnin' up!" cried Birdie in distress.

The men did not move. They looked at each other and smiled. Then Joe Slater said in a drawling voice, "We'll be over later!"

Birdie knew they would never come.

"Where's Shoestring?" she asked. She had a vague hope that

he might help her, if she begged him hard enough.

"Dunno," said Joe.

"Somewheres around," said Gus.

Sam did not speak. He just smiled.

"You're the meanest man in the world, Sam Slater!" burst out Birdie. Her anger was a flaming thing as hot as the fire itself.

"Shet your mouth, gal young un!" muttered Slater. "Speak mannerly to your elders!"

"Anybody that won't help, but leaves fire fightin' to women-folks . . ." Birdie went on.

"I'll go help!" Mrs. Slater rushed out from the door. "I'll go help my neighbors when they're in trouble!"

"Woman, you come right back here!" ordered Sam Slater. His wife turned and went obediently back into the house.

Birdie slapped her horse and rode off. "The meanest man in the world!" she kept saying. "He jest *wants* to burn us out!" Then she remembered the note. Of course that was it. *"Will git you yet iffen we got to burn you out!"* it had said. She understood now. Slater had been determined ever since the first, to drive them back to the place they had come from. He was trying to burn them out, like he said.

It was while she was galloping home that Birdie remembered the little girls. They were playing in the palmetto tunnel.

The palmetto clumps were so large and dense, they completely shut out the sun, and the children had made rooms under them. They liked to play house there, it was so shady and cozy.

They had found old boards to make seats and tables, and beds for their play-dollies. They had places to keep all their treasures—old bottles and scraps of broken glass and dishes.

Essie and Zephy Slater were there now with Dovey and Bunny.

They would not be able to see the fire or smell the smoke. The fire would trap them. The dry bristling palmetto leaves would burn like lightwood. Birdie's heart quaked. No one would think of the children. They would all be so busy fighting fire, even Buzz and Pa, when they came.

Birdie pounded Osceola and rode faster. When she reached home, she pulled up the horse and stared. The house was still standing, unharmed. The stepladder still stood by the outer wall, half of which shone pearly white in the midday sun. Pa and Buzz had come back and she saw with relief that they had the fire under control. It had moved far over to the right, beyond the farm buildings, into the scrub.

"The Slaters purely won't come, Pa!" cried Birdie. "He set the fire hisself and was tryin' to burn us out!" Then Birdie saw that the fire was burning hot and crackling furiously round the clump of palmettos, the beginning of the tunnel.

"Pa!" she screamed hoarsely. "The children! They're playin' in the palmettos!"

They all ran. Pa brought an armful of wet sacks. Buzz carried the children out of the tunnel one at a time, wet sacks thrown over them. Ma poured water on the burning roots.

Dovey and Bunny were scared but unharmed. Essie and

[154]

Zephy cried from fright. They were very dirty and black from the smoke. Birdie took them all out on the back porch and washed them clean. The fire moved on and the danger was over, though many pine trees kept burning for days and the smell of pine filled the air.

Ma sent Birdie to take the Slater girls home.

"I'll look see can I find Speckle and her biddies first," said Birdie. When she could not find them in the house or the yard, she decided to hunt for them in the woods on her way to the Slaters.

It was an impossible task to try and locate a hen and her chicks in the burned-off woods. Birdie watched until Essie and Zephy reached their front porch safely. She had no wish to go nearer their house. She never wanted to see any of the Slaters again.

She followed a pig trail, looking for Speckle. Through the woods she came upon dead snakes, small animals and ground-nesting birds that had been burned in the fire. She walked on awhile and then heard voices. A crowd of people had gathered and were talking. She hurried through the blackened grass to the place where they were. It looked familiar and yet she scarcely recognized it.

Then she saw that it was the schoolyard. There was the pump by the trough. There was the boys' baseball field. There was the rope swing under the live oak tree. But the schoolhouse was gone. It was burned to the ground. It had caught from the grass fire and was now only a heap of hot, smoking coals and ashes.

Birdie forgot the loss of hen and biddies, in the light of this new calamity. She wanted to go back to school again. She had heard that Miss Annie Laurie Dunnaway was to be the new teacher.

The people were talking about Sam Slater. Nobody said that he had started the fire. But somebody remarked that his boys had fought the man teacher and had broken up the school, because Mr. Pearce had moved away.

"I tell you what!" Birdie could not keep still, "our house was fixin' to burn up, and I rode over to Slaters' to ask 'em to come help, and they wouldn't never come! They tipped their chairs agin the wall and jest sot! Sam Slater's the meanest man in the world!"

Nobody answered her. No one gave her the support she expected. She looked around in dismay.

Then she saw the reason. There stood Shoestring. He had heard every word she said. The people looked from her to the boy, to see how he would take it.

They were cowards. She was not.

Shoestring stared fiercely at her with his black, beady eyes, but she did not care. She stared back at him.

"Now you won't mess up with no school, Jefferson Davis Slater!" she said in a good loud voice. "Nor learn to read nor write, will you?"

"No!" said Shoestring. He dropped his eyes and in his voice there was a note of sadness. "Now they ain't no more school to go to, I wisht I might could go."

[156]

CHAPTER XIII

Brown Mule

BARNEY BARNUM, the horse trader, was in the square. He attended all public gatherings and was always in town on Saturdays. A crowd had gathered round him.

"Give boot, take boot!" shouted Barney. "I'll swap, sell or buy!" He had a shaggy spotted pony on the end of his rope. "Swap, sell or buy!" he kept repeating in a loud voice.

Mr. Boyer and Birdie hurried over. Pa pulled the cow behind him.

After Semina died, Pa needed a mule badly. There was too much work for Osceola to do. The frequent trips to town alone were enough for the horse's strength. A good work mule was a necessity. So, as soon as the strawberry crop was harvested, Pa felt he could afford one. He decided to trade in a cow, and pay some cash if necessary. His fenced-in pasture was not large enough to accommodate a large herd, and he felt he had more cows than he needed. He preferred to be a farmer and not a cattleman.

Birdie looked at the horse trader's pony.

"But we want a mule!" she whispered to her father.

"You mighty right," said Pa. "But he'll trade four or five times before the day's over. We'll wait, see what comes in."

"Looka here what a nice horse," cried the horse trader. "She's a Florida-raised little horse. She's been broke a little, she can work. Last evenin' I hooked her up to that drag out there and I went round the block three times before I could stop her. I tell you, she tore out with me and nigh killed me!"

The crowd laughed.

"Swap, sell or buy!" shouted Barney.

A man leading a mule began to dicker.

"Don't you worry, she don't buck!" insisted Barney.

The man's ten-year-old son ran up, threw himself on the horse's back and tried to ride her.

"Don't get her excited now," cried Barney. "She might buck after all!"

The crowd laughed again.

"Swap, sell or buy!" called Barney.

Soon the animals changed hands. The man handed his mule to Barney, then he and his son rode off on the horse's back.

"Thank you, sir!" shouted Barney after them. "You stoled you a good horse! Who wants to swap this here little ole mule?"

❧❧❧❧❧❧❧❧❧❧❧❧❧❧❧❧❧❧❧❧❧❧❧❧❧❧

"Hit's a mule, Pa!" whispered Birdie. "Now's your chance."

"We don't want ary mule like that un, honey," said Pa, shaking his head.

"One-eyed, by Jerusalem!" cried Barney Barnum. "Goes to prove I always git the worst of the bargain." He looked the mule over. "I reckon she's moon-eyed. She can see out of her left eye—all she needs is a pair of specs. But, outside of that, she's sound. Swap, sell or buy!"

A newcomer turned in a cow and led the mule away.

"Get her out of here, hope I'll never lay eyes on her again!" called Barney. "You-all's killin' a man right now, gittin' the best of ary deal I make. Iffen you got a sick hog or cow or mule, jest leave it to home. Iffen you know your horse's fixin' to die, take it somewheres else. Don't bring it to Barney Brown to swap!"

The black cow was so thin, Barney said he could see through her. She was balky too, and had to be pulled and slapped and pushed. Barney's arguments fell on empty air, and it was some time before the cow found an owner. Then a man from Kissimmee brought up a brown mule. This time, Mr. Boyer stepped forward.

Barney began his harangue: "Work anywhere you want to put her. Six years old and I don't mean seven. She's not an outlaw, she won't fight you, kick you or bite you! Best little mule in the whole state of Floridy. Just talk to her, whisper to her and she'll do what you say. Works anywhere, not a thing wrong with her, sound as a gold doubloon!"

Boyer opened the mule's mouth and looked at her teeth.

"Have a look! Hit won't cost you nothin' extry!" shouted Barney. "Have two looks at Kissimmee, the mule! See by her teeth how young she is. I guarantee her the youngest, strongest, workingest mule in the entire United States."

The mule was a good one. Other buyers recognized it, came up and made offers. Barney stopped talking to look over the animals offered in trade. When Boyer pulled a gold piece out of his pocket and offered it to boot, besides his cow, the horse trader did not hesitate.

"Done!" he shouted. "The trade is made. Go git you a new plow, sir, run git your croppin' done, and you're a rich man!"

When Pa came away, leading a big brown mule by the rope,

❦❦❦❦❦❦❦❦❦❦❦❦❦❦❦❦❦❦❦❦❦❦❦

Birdie could not help but think of Semina. Poor, thin, bony, friendly old Semina! It would seem strange to have a brown mule instead of a white one. The new mule was strong and fat and sleek, but just as gentle. Birdie patted her on the nose. "Hello, Kissimmee!" she said. "Pa, let's call her Kissimmee, 'cause she came from there."

"Shore!" said Pa. "Mighty fine ole Indian name. Jest suits her."

They tied the mule to the back of the wagon and started for home.

"I hope Slater won't poison this mule, Pa," said Birdie.

"He better not!" said Pa. "We'll keep her locked up in the barn when we're not workin' her."

"Looks like Slater's drunk most all the time lately," said Birdie. "First he poisoned Semina, then he set the grass fire and burned the schoolhouse down. What's he fixin to do next?"

"Ary man drinks all the time is shore to come to a bad end," said Pa. "He hurts other folks, but he hurts hisself most. Iffen he don't change his ways, he'll suffer for all the harm he's done."

"You ain't fixin' to kill no more of his hogs, be you, Pa?" asked Birdie.

"Can't promise!" said Pa grimly. "He jest better not come messin' round my purty brown mule, is all I say!"

"Reckon we better not tell the Slaters we got us a new mule," said Birdie thoughtfully.

They reached home at midday and all the family came running out to meet them.

"Her name's Kissimmee!" said Birdie proudly. "She come from there, so I named her."

They crowded round the new brown mule and admired her. They all said how much fatter and younger she was than old Semina, and what a good worker she would be. Suddenly Birdie saw the little Slater girls coming toward her, out of the palmetto tunnel.

"Slaters!" she cried, pointing. She wished she had an apron on, big enough to cover the brown mule and hide her from sight. But she could only pull the mule away quickly in the direction of the barn.

"Tell them Slater gals to go along home!" she called to Dan, as she ran. But when she came back to the house, there they were, standing in the breezeway.

"I done tole you to go home," she said harshly. "Don't want you to come round here never no more."

"We come to . . ." began Essie timidly.

"Tell me one thing and mind you tell me the truth. Did you see what we brung from town?" demanded Birdie fiercely. "Did you see what I was leadin' by the rope?"

"A new mule!" said Essie.

"A brown mule, 'stid of a white one!" said Zephy.

❦❦❦❦❦❦❦❦❦❦❦❦❦❦❦❦❦❦❦❦❦❦❦❦❦

They had seen it, of course. She hadn't been quick enough to hide Kissimmee from their sight as she had hoped. Birdie leaned down, pointed her finger at them and spoke sternly.

"Don't you never tell your Pa or your Ma or anybody else we got us a new mule!" she said. "You never seen no mule at all. Hear? You don't know we got us a new one. Hear? All you know is our ole white mule is dead, and your Pa poisoned it. Hear?"

"You ain't got no mule," said Essie obediently.

"Your ole white mule is dead," said Zephy.

"Mind now! And go on home!" ordered Birdie. "Go along home and stay there. Don't you never come back again!"

But the little girls would not budge.

"We want to see your Ma," they insisted.

Birdie took them tightly by the hands and led them into the house. Mrs. Boyer was stirring up cornbread for dinner. She glanced at the girls. "Iffen hit's soap your Ma wants," she said sharply, "tell her I ain't got none till I go to town and buy me some. Iffen hit's sugar, tell her I can't spare her none, till she brings back what she borrowed before."

"She don't want no soap," said Essie.

"She don't want no sugar," said Zephy.

"What do she want then?" asked Mrs. Boyer, out of patience.

Essie swallowed hard, then she spoke as if she had learned a piece by rote: "Ma's fixin' to have a chicken pilau down on the branch." In backwoods fashion, she pronounced the word per-low. "She bids you-all to come."

[163]

❦❦❦❦❦❦❦❦❦❦❦❦❦❦❦❦❦❦❦❦❦❦❦❦

"A chicken pilau!" cried Mrs. Boyer in surprise. "You mean she's inviting us?"

"Yes, ma'am," said Essie. "Shoestring's gone around to bid all the other neighbors to come. This evenin', all evenin' and tonight, at the branch down back of our house."

"I don't understand," said Mrs. Boyer. "Your folks is mad at us. Ever since Mr. Boyer whopped Shoestring, they ain't spoke to us. Your Pa poisoned our mule. Then he refused to help us put out the grass fire, when our house like to burned up. Now you invite us to come and frolic. We purely can't."

"They jest want us to overlook all the mean things they done done to us!" broke in Birdie angrily. "We don't go to ary doin's at their house, do we?"

"Ma ain't mad at you," said Essie.

"And Pa's gone away," added Zephy. "Ma said likely he won't be back for two-three days."

"Where's he gone to?" asked Mrs. Boyer.

"We don't know," said Essie. "He always goes off when he gits rarin'."

Mrs. Boyer hesitated. What did all this mean?

"Ma thought likely you'd help her dress the chickens," said Zephy, " 'count of she's got all of them to do."

"All of them? What did she kill all of 'em for? Don't she know how many folks is comin'?" asked Mrs. Boyer, more and more puzzled.

"Well," said Essie, "Pa shot the heads offen all of Ma's chickens and . . ."

"What!" exclaimed Mrs. Boyer.

"So Ma's fixin' to have a chicken pilau!" added Zephy.

"What did he do that for?" gasped Mrs. Boyer.

"He was drunk," said Essie. She hung her head, ashamed.

"He practiced hittin' the mark, to show what a good shot he was, even when he was drunk," said Zephy. "And now Ma ain't got no more chickens."

"And no more egg money," added Mrs. Boyer.

"Likely he was drunk when he poisoned Semina," said Birdie.

"I reckon so," said Ma. "That pore woman!" She opened the oven door and shoved the cornbread inside. She turned to the girls. "Tell your Ma we're shore obliged, and will be glad to come."

The chicken pilau was a gay and happy occasion. The Tatums, the Marshes and the Dorseys came, besides the Boyers.

It was pleasantly cool under the trees along by the trickling stream which was always spoken of as "the branch." The men cleared an open space and built lightwood fires and put on great kettles of water to heat. The women dressed the chickens, cut them up and boiled them. They put on rice to cook. Later the chickens and rice were cooked together with rich seasoning to make the favorite backwoods dish—chicken pilau. While the meal was in preparation, the men went off hunting and fishing, and the children played games. Lank Tatum brought his mouth organ and furnished music for the dancing that followed after dark.

Through it all Mrs. Slater was as quiet and easy as could be.

She told everybody what her husband had done, and they admired her for her spirit. Slater's absence was a great relief.

After the others had gone, Mrs. Slater fell into Mrs. Boyer's arms and cried a little.

"There, there now, hit's all over," said Mrs. Boyer, "and they all done had a good time."

"Nothin' like a frolic," said Mrs. Slater tearfully, "to ease the spirit."

"I'd a buried the dead chickens, had it been me," said Mrs. Boyer, "and not let anybody know."

"Hit seemed so wasteful," said Mrs. Slater. "Most of them hens layin' too. But when he gits to rompin' and rarin', I don't pay no mind. Then purty soon he goes off to git sobered up."

"Mis' Slater," said Mrs. Boyer, "I'm right sorry 'bout them hogs. Bihu's someways hot-tempered and he was mad. But he didn't belong to kill them three hogs of your'n. That's what started all the trouble, I reckon."

The women sat on buckskin rockers on the front porch, Mrs. Slater with her baby on her lap and Birdie leaned against her mother's knee. The whippoorwills were calling and the moon shone with a clear brilliance.

"Things is goin' from bad to worse," sighed Mrs. Slater. "Iffen hit ain't one thing, hit's two—he's drinkin' so much."

"He won't stop?" asked Mrs. Boyer.

"Nothin' can't stop ary habit like that . . ."

"Exceptin' to take the liquor away. Where do he get it?"

"The Lord only knows," said Mrs. Slater. "Spends all his

[166]

money for it. Never gives none to his family. Do our clothes git wore out more, they'll fall off us in rags. I been usin' my egg money for calico for my dresses and overalls for the boys, and now hit's gone."

"This can't go on," said Mrs. Boyer. "Him drinkin' all the time, and our men quarrelin' over hogs and cows. We're neighbors and we belong to live peaceable."

"You mighty right," sighed Mrs. Slater.

"Did the young uns tell you how we saved 'em from the grass fire, ma'am?" asked Birdie.

Mrs. Slater had heard nothing about it, so Mrs. Boyer told her the story. She rocked back and forth in her chair. "I'm shore obliged," she said. Then she began to cry. "He done set that fire to burn you folkses out and send you back to Caroliny where you come from."

"I mean!" said Mrs. Boyer. "We like to burnt up, but we ain't goin' back."

They rocked awhile in silence.

"I hear they're fixin' to hold Camp Meetin' down to Ellis's Picnic Grounds," said Mrs. Slater. "I'd admire to hear some of the preachin'. There's nothin' I relish more'n a good noisy sermon. You reckon we might could go?"

"Why yes," said Mrs. Boyer. "It would pleasure us, too. Do you have no other way to go, we'll take you-all with us."

"Iffen Sam would only go too . . ." began Mrs. Slater.

"Hit would do him a heap of good," added Mrs. Boyer.

"Ever since I bought me that Bible from the Bible-sellin'

feller," said Mrs. Slater, "I been thinkin' we belong to git more religion."

"We all belong to git more," said Mrs. Boyer, "to learn how to love our neighbor."

"Sam, he sometimes goes to the church doin's," said Mrs. Slater, "but he don't pay no mind to the preacher."

"What he needs is . . ." began Mrs. Boyer.

"A change of heart," added Mrs. Slater. She paused, then she began to sing an old Florida lullaby to her baby. Her soft thin voice melted into the stillness of the night:

> " 'Hush, little baby, don't say a word,
> Papa's gonna buy you a mockin'bird;
> If that mockin'bird don't sing,
> Papa's gonna buy you a diamond ring;
> If that diamond ring turns to brass,
> Papa's gonna buy you a lookin' glass;
> If that lookin' glass gets broke,
> Papa's gonna buy you a billygoat;
> If that billygoat runs away,
> Papa's gonna buy you a horse and dray.' "

CHAPTER XIV

The Preacher

NOTHING was heard from the Slaters for about a week. Then one night, Birdie woke with a start. She heard a familiar voice in the kitchen. It sounded like Shoestring Slater, but what could he want in the middle of the night? Birdie listened.

"Ma's sick and wants you to come quick." He was not asking Mrs. Boyer to come, he was demanding it.

A ray from the kitchen lamp made a path of light on the bedroom floor. Birdie listened.

"Ma's got a fever and the young uns are ailin' too," said the boy. "They cry all the time. Pa ain't come home and I don't know what to do."

Birdie jumped up. She looked through the door and saw that

her mother was already dressed and was putting some things in a basket. A flickering lantern hung from Shoestring's hand.

"I'll go with you, Ma," said Birdie.

"Well, hurry then." Ma did not glance up.

"I don't like night-goin'," said Shoestring. "Hit's mighty dark and lonesome-like in them pines."

"We ain't afeard," said Birdie.

It was too dark to take the short cut through the palmetto tunnel. They went the long way round, through the scrub and the piney woods. Shoestring led the way along a pig trail, swinging his lantern, while Mrs. Boyer and Birdie followed close behind. There was no moon, and the lantern sent long moving shadows off into the surrounding blackness. Strange

❧❧❧❧❧❧❧❧❧❧❧❧❧❧❧❧❧❧❧❧❧❧❧❧❧❧❧❧❧❧❧

night noises fell on their ears—chirpings and rustlings.

The Slater baby was crying hard when they got there. Essie and Zephy were awake and fretful. They were feverish, too, like their mother.

"We done brung so much trouble on you already . . ." began Mrs. Slater in a feeble voice, from the bed.

"No time to think of that now," answered Mrs. Boyer.

"Hit pulled my heart out nearly, to have to send for you," added Mrs. Slater, "but I done knowed ye'd come."

Mrs. Boyer walked back and forth between the two beds in the front room, doing what she could to ease the sick patients. Then she went to the kitchen to make some mullein tea and other healing brews.

Shoestring fell asleep on a pallet bed in the little lean-to.

"Is Mis' Slater fixin' to die, Ma?" asked Birdie, wide-eyed.

"The Lord only knows!" answered her mother. "She's plumb sick and needs lookin' after. We'll have to stay right on. Dixie can look out for the folks at home."

All that first night and for several more, Mrs. Boyer stayed up, caring for the sick woman and her children. She and Birdie snatched brief naps when they could. But Mrs. Slater did not die. She began to respond to the medicine, care and nourishing food. The little girls improved rapidly and soon were themselves again. But the baby continued fretful and puny, refusing to eat.

The furnishings of the house were very meager. Besides the beds, there was one small table and one bureau. Clothes hung from wooden pegs in the wall. The kitchen had a fireplace for cooking, a large oilcloth-covered table and a safe for food. There were two frying pans, a few kettles and some crocks and dishes.

A large picture hung on the wall beside Mrs. Slater's bed. It was in a brown oval frame. It showed a man in overalls, wearing a black felt hat. He held a fat baby in his arms.

"Hit's Sam!" Mrs. Slater pointed to it with pride. "Holdin' the baby."

Mrs. Boyer studied the picture. "Ain't it wonderful? Hit don't resemble him a mite!"

"Wal—no," drawled Mrs. Slater. "That artist feller drawed it."

"The Lightnin' Artist," asked Birdie, "who painted pictures in the square in town? I seen him paint a road and a hill once, fast as lightnin'."

"Very same one," said Mrs. Slater. "He come one evenin' jest before dark and asked could he spend the night. Sam was feelin' good and said yes. In the mornin' he drawed the picture for the breakfast I give him. He drawed it with a black crayon. He 'lowed he draws cows better'n men and babies. But we thought hit was mighty handsome."

"Shore is!" agreed Mrs. Boyer. She was glad to see that Mrs. Slater had one thing to take pride in.

"He drawed pine trees behind, 'cause we live in the piney woods," added Mrs. Slater. "I jest admire to lie here and look at it. I never stayed in bed so long before. I feel right lazy."

[172]

"You deserve a good long rest," said Mrs. Boyer. "You been a mighty sick woman."

"I'd be in the cemetery now, were it not for you, ma'am," said Mrs. Slater tearfully.

"Now, now," laughed Mrs. Boyer, "your time ain't come yet. You got these here young uns to raise."

"I made some blackberry jell and I was fixin' to give you some that day I first come to see you. . . ." She paused. "I did so want to like you, but it seemed like I jest couldn't . . ."

Mrs. Boyer patted her hand to comfort her. "We're good friends now," she said.

"You're so easy to neighbor with," said Mrs. Slater.

Birdie found the little girls friendly again too. She showed them how to play games and she kept them quiet while their mother slept. She helped with the baby. When it cried, she rocked it in the rocking chair on the porch. She brought milk from home for the baby to drink, and soon it began to smile and grow fat again.

Shoestring went about the house with closed lips. He spoke only when spoken to, and then in the briefest words. But he helped in every way he could. He kept the woodbox filled, the porch and kitchen swept. He carried pails of water from the sinkhole.

One afternoon late, a man arrived on horseback. He had been riding a long way, and was dusty and tired. He was tall and thin, with a shock of black hair. His eyes were fiery, his cheeks sunken.

"Hit's the preacher from Tallahassee!" whispered Mrs. Slater, glancing from her bed out of the window. "He's one of them Camp Meetin' preachers, the same one who come last year. Lawzy, me sick and all, what will we do?"

"Bid him welcome, of course," said Mrs. Boyer, drying her hands on her apron. "Howdy!" she said, as the preacher came up on the porch.

"Howdy, ma'am!" The man doffed his hat. "I've come a powerful long ways since mornin'. Do you reckon I might rest here, ma'am?"

Mrs. Boyer took him in to see Mrs. Slater. The sick woman flushed with excitement.

"Did I know you was a-comin', Brother . . ."

"Jackson, ma'am."

"Did I know you was a-comin', Brother Jackson," said Mrs. Slater, "I'd a killed us a chicken for dinner." Then she bit her lips, remembering she had no more chickens to kill.

"I'm so hungry, I can eat most anything, ma'am," said the man.

Mrs. Boyer gave Mrs. Slater a meaningful look, and slipped out of the room.

"We jest got common rations," said Mrs. Slater, "but you're plumb welcome to set down with us." Then she added, "I been so sick, I thought I'd never over it."

"Would you like me to pray for you, ma'am?"

Mrs. Boyer closed the door quietly, called Shoestring and sent him on an errand. When he returned later, he brought with him two young chickens from the Boyer flock and a basket containing a white linen tablecloth and other necessities.

"You want me to chop their heads off, ma'am?" asked the boy.

"I'd be proud if you did," said Mrs. Boyer.

The dinner which Mrs. Boyer cooked was delicious, with fried chicken and all the trimmings—turnip and mustard greens, sweet potatoes, peach preserves, blackberry jelly and pickles, grits and gravy, biscuit and crackling cornbread. The table in the front room was set close to Mrs. Slater's bed. Brother Jackson and Mrs. Boyer faced each other across the white cloth and Mrs. Slater, propped up with pillows, sat between them.

The children waited in the kitchen behind the closed door. They were instructed to be very quiet, so as not to be heard. The walls between the rooms were rough plank partitions up to the height of the eaves. The attic space under the gabled roof was not floored, but left open for circulation of air.

"We want to go in! We want to go in!" cried Essie and Zephy.

"Not when the preacher's here," scolded Birdie. "Young uns never eat with the preacher!" She pulled them away from the door.

"He said he was so hungry he could eat anything," groaned Shoestring in an undertone. "How 'bout me? I'm hungry as a woods cow that can't find no grass!"

"Wait till he gits done," said Birdie.

[175]

"All we git is what's left over!" complained Shoestring. "I'm hungry as a hound dog on the scent of a rabbit. I'm so hungry I could eat a handful of them turpentine chips."

"Here! Take this!" Birdie handed him a cold biscuit.

He threw it into the fireplace. "*Cold* biscuit!" he sniffed. "I'm sick and tired of cold biscuit! They belong to be hot!"

They listened to the subdued murmur of voices in the front room.

"Can't see why *he* should git all the chicken!" said Shoestring.

"He's the preacher, that's why," said Birdie.

"I want to see how much he's et," said the boy.

"What you fixin' to do?" asked Birdie in sudden alarm.

Shoestring did not answer. He stepped on a chair, then on the kitchen table and from there onto one of the wooden clothes pegs. He grasped the beam across the top of the partition, and slowly chinned himself. He put his arms over and hung on. With wide open eyes, he stared down on the table in the next room and the three people eating there.

"You better not, Shoestring Slater!" scolded Birdie in a loud whisper. "You jest better not do that. Do-o-o-n't git up there!"

But the boy did not hear her. He only stared at the splendid white table in the next room. He stared at the platter which had been heaped so high a short time before. He stared at the preacher's plate covered with chicken bones. He saw a drumstick in the man's hand.

A loud exclamation burst from his lips: "Lordy! He's takened

[178]

the last piece and he's eatin' it! There ain't none left!"

Three pairs of horrified eyes glanced up from the table.

"Take that boy out and whop him!" said the preacher angrily. "That'll learn him to be mannerly!"

Shoestring let go his hold and slid precipitately down the kitchen side of the partition.

"You gone and went and done it!" cried Birdie. "You gone and spoiled it all!"

When he reached the floor, Shoestring wheeled and made a beeline for the back door.

"Your Ma'll take a bresh to you," cried Birdie. "You better run to save your hide!"

Essie and Zephy began to wail because there was no chicken left. Mrs. Boyer came out to quiet them. Mrs. Slater called: "Catch that boy and whop him good, Mis' Boyer!"

Only the preacher remained unruffled. He asked for the Bible. Mrs. Boyer found it on a window sill and handed it to him.

"I bought it from that Bible-sellin' feller," explained Mrs. Slater. "I declare to goodness, looks like hit got rained on. Don't know who put it on the window sill."

It was dusk-dark now and the room was filled with shadows. Mrs. Boyer brought the kitchen lamp and set it on the little table. The preacher turned the leaves and read in a hearty voice while Birdie and the little girls stood near and listened.

"Let us pray," he said.

They fell to their knees and bowed their heads. "We thank

thee, Lord, for all thy blessings . . . quench not the spirit in us, keep it gushing up like an artesian well . . . O Lord, give us such power that the old temptations look silly . . . no more shall we indulge in intoxicating liquor, backbiting, gossip or excessive anger. . . . Teach us to love our neighbor as ourselves. . . ."

Mrs. Boyer gave the girls some supper, but Shoestring did not appear. She made up a fresh pallet bed on the kitchen floor for the preacher. The next morning, after a hearty breakfast, he invited the women to bring their families and attend Camp Meeting the following week. Then he rode away, rested and refreshed.

"Where's that young limb o' Satan?" cried Mrs. Slater. "I'll learn him to be mannerly!"

Shoestring was afraid to come to the house, but hunger drove him as far as the back door. He had had little food during his mother's illness and the lack of supper the night before proved the last straw. Birdie hid cornbread and biscuit under her apron and took them out to him.

"I'm hungry as an ole 'gator opening his big jaws to swaller a hog whole!" said Shoestring. "Git me more! Git me more 'fore I fall in my tracks!" He did not object to cold biscuit, but gobbled them greedily.

Birdie came back the second time but her hands were empty. "Come git it yourself," she said.

"But Ma'll whop me," wailed Shoestring. Only too well did he understand how he had shamed his mother before the preacher.

❦❦❦❦❦❦❦❦❦❦❦❦❦❦❦❦❦❦❦❦❦❦❦❦❦❦❦

"You're too big to git whopped," said Birdie, "and besides, your Ma's sick in bed."

"She'll git your Ma to do it then," whined the boy.

"You shore deserve it," said Birdie. "Come git it over with."

Shoestring stared at her as if the idea were a new one. He edged inside the door and eyed the food on the breakfast table. But he did not move toward it. When Mrs. Boyer came in from the bedroom, he spoke to her.

"Whop me, ma'am!" he said. "I'd be proud to git it over with, so I can eat. I'm as hungry as a razorback 'at can't find no palmetto roots."

Mrs. Boyer looked him over. "I can't whop you," she said.

"You mean Ma can't, 'cause she's sick."

"I mean I can't," she said. "You're too big. I'm too tired from nursin' your Ma to undertake sich a hard job as that."

The boy's eyes filled with tears. "I near about forgot . . ." he said.

He crumpled up on a chair and began to sob. Mrs. Boyer patted him on the back. "There, there now," she said, "you're jest hungry, that's all. You ain't had a square meal in a week."

"I'm shore obliged, ma'am!" The boy found his tongue at last. "I'm shore obliged for all you done done for Ma and the young uns. I'm plumb sorry for all the trouble us Slaters has made for you-all. . . ."

"There now, son," said Mrs. Boyer. "Come eat."

Birdie filled his plate with white bacon and grits three times before Shoestring's hunger was satisfied.

"Taste good?" she asked. "Good as fried chicken?"

"I mean!" he said, glancing out of the window. Then he jumped up. "Golly! There's Pa back!"

Sam Slater stalked in, followed by Gus and Joe. "Breakfast ready?" he cried.

Then he saw that the woman leaning over the fireplace was not his wife, and that the girl who was washing dishes was not one of his daughters.

"Jerusalem!" He spat angrily on the hearth. "Whar's Azalee Slater, my wife, and the young uns? What you-all doin' here, messin' in other folkses kitchens?"

Before Mrs. Boyer had time to answer, he burst out: "Git on outen here! I won't have ary Boyer in my house. Git outen here before I throw ye out!"

[182]

"Better go see Ma first, Pa!" begged Shoestring, in a low but firm voice. "She's in bed, sick."

Slater looked at his son in surprise.

Shoestring stood up straight and tall, and explained all that had happened during his father's absence. Sam Slater's anger faded and his assurance wilted away. Gus and Joe slumped in slat-backed chairs and patted their hounds. Then Sam Slater went into his wife's room.

When he came out again, he offered his hand to Mrs. Boyer. "I hate to be beholden to ary Boyer," he said, "but I'm shore obliged to ye for savin' my wife's life, and the young uns too."

CHAPTER XV

New Organ

"IS it true," asked Birdie, "that your Pa got converted?"

"Yes," said Shoestring. The boy's face lighted up with happiness. "He's a different man. I won't need to be ashamed of him no more."

"I'm proud!" said Birdie. "For you and for your Ma and for the young uns."

"It wouldn't never have happened, iffen you folkses hadn't come to live in the ole Roddenberry house," said the boy.

"I'm proud we came then," said Birdie.

"To think it was Brother Jackson who done it!" exclaimed Shoestring. "I'd set and watch him eat two chickens at one meal ary time now and not begrudge him a bite!"

"I watched him at Camp Meeting," said Birdie. "He worked on your Pa for a long time. I thought he'd never be able to do it."

Shoestring continued: "That day when he et all the chicken, Ma told him how Pa got drunk all the time, and he promised he'd pray extry hard for him."

"And so he did," added Birdie softly.

The Boyer and Slater wagons had come home together from the Camp Meeting at Ellis's Picnic Grounds, and the two families were gathered on the Boyer front porch. Birdie and Shoe-string sat down on the steps.

"Glory hallelujah!" cried Sam Slater, throwing his hat in the air. "I'm a changed man! A happy man for the first time in my life!"

"Brother Jackson shore is a powerful preacher," said Mrs. Boyer.

"To touch the heart of a hardened sinner like me," added Slater.

"I mean no offense . . ." began Mrs. Boyer.

"But hit's true, ain't it?" said Slater gently. "My heart was hard as a rock. Now 'tis soft as mud. I'll never be the same again, thank God."

"How did it happen, Sam?" asked Boyer. "Tell us about it."

Sam Slater grew thoughtful, then he spoke: "When I come home and found my wife and young uns had been lyin' at death's door, I begun to think. Did I not have kind, forgivin' neighbors, they'd a been dead. Then the very next night I got sick myself, and thought I was fixin' to die. So I decided I'd better start livin' different. But it was Brother Jackson who pointed out the error of my ways. He told me the harm of drinkin' liquor, and of swearin' and backbitin', gossip and anger.

So when the spirit come upon me, I was ready. My heart was changed. I'm fixin' to lead the good life right on."

"Praise God!" cried the women.

"Glory be to God!" added the men.

"You won't never get drunk no more, Pa?" asked Essie.

"And shoot the chickens' heads off, Pa?" asked Zephy.

"No, young uns, I won't!" said Sam Slater. He took the two little girls in his arms and held them close. "And I hope to be a good neighbor right on, too. A good father and a good neighbor."

Mrs. Slater and Mrs. Boyer smiled happily at each other.

Slater turned to Boyer. "You ain't the only one to fence in the land," he said.

"How's that?" asked Boyer.

"Phosphate company's leased a whole stretch north of here and they're fencin' it in," said Slater. "Cattlemen don't like it. They've always had that land for their cattle to run over."

"More squabbles then, I reckon," said Boyer, smiling.

"I reckon so," said Slater.

"Times are bound to change," said Boyer. "Open Range can't last forever in Florida."

"Further south it will. Plenty of open land down there— that's where cattle raising will flourish. One of my cows got bogged down in that phosphate mud!" said Slater, laughing. "They paid damages—twice what she was worth."

"I hope they won't come too near my land," said Boyer.

[186]

"Phosphate's used for making fertilizer and other things, but the way they mine the stuff out of the ground—piling up mountains of dirt and running ditches everywhere, and layin' their railroads with engines a-tootin' and whistlin', and building all them houses—I don't like it. It ruins all the farms near by."

Slater shook his head. "Hit 'ain't good for the farmer nor the cattleman neither. They've leased most of the land my cows run over for pasture."

"That makes it mighty bad for you, if they fence in your range," said Boyer. "What will you do?"

"Sell out," said Slater. "Can't do nothin' to stop it. Citrus people are fencing, too. Got to quit the cattle business, I reckon." A week before, Slater would have ranted with furious anger. Now he spoke quietly and peaceably. Every one noticed the change.

"What you fixin' to do?" asked Boyer.

"Take a job with the phosphate company, I reckon!" Slater laughed heartily. "Ain't nothin' else to do. Hear them loud booms goin' off early every mornin'? They're dynamitin' the stuff out of the ground. I went over to tell 'em what I thought of 'em for fencin' my cows out, and I come home with the job of dynamiter! Hit will jest suit me. Grandpa was an old Indian fighter in the Seminole War. He liked nothin' better than firin' off a gun, and I favor him in most ways. I reckon hit'll jest about suit me to touch off a fuse in them pits, then run as fast as I can, and listen to it go BOOM and blow the whole place up!"

[187]

Everybody laughed.

"I can't say I'll be sorry to see the last of that herd of cows of your'n!" said Boyer.

"Birdie," said Mrs. Boyer, "go fetch the strawberry wine."

Shoestring followed her to the kitchen. She filled the glasses and the boy placed them on the tray.

"I'll tell you something," Shoestring confided, "I'm fixin' to go to school once the new schoolhouse is built."

"To learn to read and write?" asked Birdie in astonishment. "Now, I think that's just plumb good!"

"Yes," said Shoestring. "Pa said he made a mistake to take Gus and Joe out of school, and he wants me to git a little book-larnin'. Pa 'lows if I'm smart enough, I might could git to be state senator or leastways county commissioner!"

"I'm shore proud to hear it," said Birdie. "I'll help you with your lessons."

When they passed the strawberry wine around, Mrs. Slater spoke up: "Some day we'll make our own strawberry wine."

"You fixin' to . . ." began Mrs. Boyer.

"Raise strawberries? Yes," said Mrs. Slater. "With Pa at the phosphate company and no cattle to trample things over, the boys will put out the crops for me and soon we'll be sellin' things like you-all. We're studyin' to put out a grove of them new seedless grapefruit too."

Mrs. Boyer glanced at the baby sleeping on Mrs. Slater's lap. "You'll keep cows enough to have milk for the young uns?"

"Shore will!" said Mrs. Slater. "I don't want 'em to grow up

[188]

❦❦❦❦❦❦❦❦❦❦❦❦❦❦❦❦❦❦❦❦❦❦❦❦❦❦❦

so puny lookin'. I want 'em to be strong and healthy."

The next time the cow buyer came through on his way from Jacksonville to Tampa, he stopped at the Slaters. Buzz and Dan Boyer had gone on the cow hunt with the Slater boys and had rounded up the cattle for the last time.

Birdie and Dovey watched the long line of cattle drive past their house. Shoestring dashed by on his cowhorse, the sharp cracks of his long whip sounding like shots from a gun. He pulled up only long enough to say: "I'm shore proud to get shet of these here cows!" Then he was gone.

It was several months before the new schoolhouse was re-built on the site of the old. It was a great improvement, with weather-boarded instead of planked walls, new seats and desks, a table and chair for the teacher, and glass sashes in the windows. The new teacher was Miss Annie Laurie Dunnaway.

It was a proud moment for Birdie when she presented Miss Dunnaway with a bunch of red roses, and introduced Shoestring Slater. It was a proud moment, but an awkward one.

"This here is Shoestring . . ." she began. "Oh, no, I mean . . ."

"My name's Jefferson Davis Slater," said the boy. "I come to git book-larnin'."

"You are one of the Slaters?" asked Miss Dunnaway. In her eyes there came a frightened look. "They told me the Slater boys had left school. Was it you and your brothers who . . ."

"Gus and Joe whopped the man teacher," said Shoestring, dropping his eyes. "I wasn't in school then."

[189]

"But Shoestring . . . I mean, Jeff's different!" broke in Birdie. "He ain't rough and wild like Gus and Joe."

"You must say 'isn't' not 'ain't,' Berthenia," corrected Miss Dunnaway.

"He isn't rough," said Birdie. "He won't make ary trouble for you, Teacher."

" 'Any' trouble, not 'ary,' " said Miss Dunnaway.

"I won't make you no trouble," said Shoestring, looking up at her, "iffen you jest larn me to read and write."

" 'Any' trouble, not 'no' trouble, Jefferson. And 'if,' not 'iffen'. 'Teach' me, not 'larn' me. That's fine. I'm proud to welcome a peaceable Slater to my school."

"I can stay then?" asked the boy, twisting his black felt hat awkwardly.

🌷🌷🌷🌷🌷🌷🌷🌷🌷🌷🌷🌷🌷🌷🌷🌷🌷🌷🌷🌷🌷🌷🌷🌷🌷🌷

"Yes, you may, Jefferson," said Miss Dunnaway. She showed him where to put his hat and dinner pail, and led him to his seat.

There was no organ at the school for Miss Dunnaway to play, but soon she was leading the children in singing, and their happy voices rang out through the silence of the piney woods, where only the shy woods creatures could hear.

When Birdie came home from school that evening, she was not prepared for the surprise that awaited her. She knew her father and mother had gone to town that day, but she was so busy thinking of school that she had not even wondered why Shoestring and Essie and Zephy and Dovey all came home with her and followed her up the porch steps. There was so much to tell about the first day of school.

But they did not tell it after all, for there on the breezeway stood the surprise. It was a beautiful parlor organ, with elaborate scroll work, shiny ivory keys, many stops and two foot pedals. A stool with a fringed velvet top stood in front of it.

"An organ!" cried Birdie. "Oh, I always wanted one!"

"Golly!" cried Shoestring.

"Looky! Looky!" cried the little girls.

"Ma, Ma!" cried Birdie. "Here's a organ! Where did it come from?"

But Ma did not answer. She was not there, nor Pa, nor Dixie, nor any of the rest of the family. Birdie wondered where they all were. The organ must have come from town, so they must have returned.

Birdie could not wait. She sat down on the beautiful stool.

[191]

She touched the stops. She laid her fingers on the ivory keys. She pressed them gently, but no music came.

"Hit don't play!" she cried in distress.

"Pump the pedals up and down with your feet," said Shoestring. "Ain't you see Miss Dunnaway do it in church?"

Birdie began to pump, pushing one pedal down and then the other. She began to play with one finger. The tones were soft and sweet. She pumped harder. They grew louder. She used two fingers, then all five.

"I jest wisht I could make me a purty tune," she said.

"Why, Berthenia Lou Boyer!" Dixie came up on the back porch with Bunny. "You darsen't touch it. Ma ain't said you might could."

Birdie lifted her hands in dismay. "What's it for then?"

"You don't belong to touch it till Ma and Pa come," said Dixie.

Suddenly they were all there. Ma stood beside her. Dan and Buzz peeped in through the kitchen door. And Pa, who was washing his face on the back porch, put his head around the corner and laughed. They had heard Birdie playing.

Pa came out. "Strawberry Girl done worked so hard on the strawberries," he said, "we made a nice surprise for her."

"Is it for me?" asked Birdie.

"Yes," said Ma, "for Strawberry Girl and for all of us."

"But Ma," cried Birdie, "I purely can't make me a purty tune! I thought it would be so easy."

"Let's hear you try," said Pa.

[192]

Birdie pumped and pounded the keys again.

"Sounds terrible," said Pa, looking at Ma. "Reckon there's anything we can do about it, wife?"

Ma smiled. "How about takin' lessons from Miss Dunnaway?"

"Oh, Pa! Oh, Ma! I might could?"

"Yes," they said. "We been studyin' on it for a long time."

"Golly!" said Shoestring. "When you get big, likely you'll play the organ in church!"

"I hope so," said Birdie.

"Play for us, wife," said Pa to Ma.

Ma sat down and played a pretty tune.

"Why Ma! How do you do it? When did you learn?" cried Birdie.

"I takened lessons way back in Caroliny when I was a young un," said Ma, "and I ain't forgot yet. Hit makes me plumb happy to put my fingers on an organ again." She looked at Pa and they smiled.

Then Ma played a hymn tune and they all crowded round the new organ and sang together:

> "O Beulah land, sweet Beulah land,
> As on thy highest mount I stand,
> I look away across the sea
> Where mansions are prepared for me
> And view the shining glory-shore:
> My heaven, my home forevermore."